Season 70 Episode 2 Mia

By

Kayla Renee

Season 70 Episode 2 Mia

Book Two

Text Copyright 2024 by Kayla Renee

This is a work of fiction.

Cover artist: Sheri S

Published by Kayla Renee

Dystopian, fantasy, action.

Special thanks to those who worked on this book with me, from my mother, who provided valuable feedback, to my line editor, Kelly Scriven.

"This was the start of something new."
Kayla Renee

Table of Contents

Chapter 1

A hand clamped tight against her mouth. The meaty fingers pressed grim into her lips. Mia struggled, jabbing her elbow into the soft spot between the ribs and stomach of the man holding her. He grunted as another hand wrapped around her waist, pulling her backwards, down, into a musty stench-filled alleyway.

"Mia!"

Eli's cry came from the sunny sidewalk she had just vacated. She writhed, needing to get the hand off of her mouth. The man holding her pressed her body up against a car, one hot from the sun. The sound of its door opening reached her ears, and all at once she was staring at the ceiling of a high-tech car. The door slamming shut behind her as the man made his way to the controller's seat. She sat up, her flight or fight response taking over as the tires squealed. The car lurched forward, causing a gasp to escape her lips.

A police-like-barrier kept her from her captor. His muscles bulged, sweat causing his white tank top to cling to his back like a sticker. The man controlled the car with the mind reader attached onto his balding head as he drove by his thoughts. Mia glanced back just in time to see Eli jumping out of the way as the car shot out of the alleyway, his face that of a wild rabbit's. Mia turned in her seat again to see her friends Harper, Kayla, Joseph, Travis, and Silvia staring after the car in shock. The car squealed around a corner and her friends were gone, out of sight. The car hummed as it picked up speed, veering around corner after corner.

"What do you want with me?" she asked.

No response.

"What do you want with me?"

The man remained silent as the car sped onward. Mia's eyes wandered the compartment, taking in every nook and cranny, every possible place she could find. There was always the chance of a secret exit. *In a high-tech vehicle like this? Really?* she asked herself, appalled that she would even consider the possibility of escape. But there was always a way. She had learned that Behind The Wall. There was always a way around a problem, from a break in the wall to an unexpected friendship with the enemy. There would be a way, one way or another—no pun, but a pun, intended. She needed to remain calm.

Her eyes wandered to the front of the car to see the driver, his head firmly attached to the driver's thought technology. She vaguely understood it when she asked someone about them, but the technology appeared to read people's minds and drove the car as such.

The car jerked around a corner, causing Mia's heart to thump hard. Mia took a slow breath. She had to remain calm.

She ran her fingers along the neatly stitched thread of the leather backseat.

"What do you want with me?" she asked again, her eyes sliding to the windows, where she could see the city flashing by so fast things were a blur.

The man jerked the car sharply to the left, causing her to slide into the passenger-side door.

"What do you want with me?" she demanded.

The man glanced into the rearview mirror, and Mia was struck by his piercing eyes the color of dappled stone.

"So?" She let her back press into the clean leather seat.

The man's eyes flicked back to the road, and he sped up faster, causing her heart to leap into her throat.

She was used to being fast. She was good at being fast. Being fast was her blessing, but when she wasn't in control… When she didn't control every movement and motion, it caused her head to begin to spin.

She glanced behind the car. Her eyes scanned the sidewalk quickly, but she didn't see anybody she knew. There was a large dog bounding down the sidewalk, one who looked a little familiar, but that was all. She faced the front again, her stomach churning slightly with all the turns and speed.

A truck's horn blasted at the electric car as it cut the truck off, causing it to slam on the brakes and skid back and forth.

Mia slid to the floor, her hands exploring underneath the seats, trying to find a secret lever or anything that might help her escape. There had to be something. But there was nothing. She sat up again and tugged on the passenger door handles, but they had been locked.

Giving up for the moment, she slid back into her seat, trying her best to act like she was not getting nervous. She was totally fine. She was not beginning to panic whatsoever. She was always calm, never afraid. Until now ... but that was beside the point.

"Let me go." She stopped, thinking. "Please," she tried.

Not a peep out of the man.

After a few more moments of squealing around corners and a sudden slamming on the breaks, the car entered a dilapidated garage outside of town. There were overturned metal trash cans scattered everywhere. The cement floor had splashes of old paint staining it.

Mia's eyes flicked all around, assessing her new situation. *Could she possibly run and escape from here?* Another man appeared from behind a large dumpster, and the driver got out, slamming the door of the car and walking over to him. This new man had curly black hair, and he was taller than the muscular captor but still looked strong. His hair was swept to the side as if he had run gel through his silver hair. His shoulders seemed more buff than they should be to match the rest of his frame. The two conferred with each other, sending glances her way.

Mia pressed herself against the seat, letting her chest heave up and down as she slid closer to the furthest door. She leaned against it, the plastic of the door handle poking into her back.

The men slowly approached her. The one with the stone-colored eyes stared deep into her eyes, as if he were a predator animal about to pounce on a deer.

Harper! Harper loved those wildlife documentaries that we watched together.

The man with the stone eyes tugged on the passenger door's handle across the car from her, and the door cracked open.

Mia's eyes flitted to the man's face. Her eyes grew wide, pretending to plead.

"L-let me g-go, please," she stuttered. She lifted a hand, letting it shake as if she were terrified, her chest continuing to heave up and down, up and down.

"It's okay, chicky," the man said, opening the door a little bit more.

Just one more moment...

"I-I'm scared," she whimpered.

"I know, ducky," the man crooned, his deep voice shaking her firm foundation, making it a little harder to ignore the fear thrashing about inside her.

"P-please just don't hurt me..." She inched towards him.

"How could I ever?" the man asked, running his hand through his hair and opening the door up all the way.

Mia bolted, her world becoming a blur as it did when she ran. She raced towards the car door, gaining speed until—*crunch!*

Mia screamed, collapsing on the cement floor, clutching her leg. The man had slammed the car door on it before she could escape..

Mia watched as the two men convened on her and tugged her up. Her breath was now really coming out quickly, not on her orders but against. The fear mounting within her was close to panic. Mia never allowed herself to panic, but now... Now was something different.

The men dragged her towards a white, mud-splattered door. Mia didn't want to know what was behind it; if her captors wanted her there, it could not be a good place.

She wriggled, writhing, attempting to get out of their grasp. The men only tightened their holds upon her, their grips sending pain down her arms. Mia dropped her legs, letting her full weight hang in the men's hands.

The men grunted in annoyance.

"You little—" the man with black hair grumbled, hoisting her back up. Her shoulders screamed as they supported her weight. She would not cooperate with these men. She snapped at the buff man's hand.

"Knock it off, chicky," the man said, swatting at her with his free hand.

The three made it to the mud-splattered door. The buff man reached out a large hand, closed his fingers around the rusted gold handle, and turned.

Mia's heart screamed to get out of her chest.

The door opened to blackness. Mia wasn't afraid of the dark. She wasn't. But this… She struggled violently, kicking at the new man's legs with her good leg. She wouldn't go through—

The men thrust her forward. The door slammed shut, swallowing Mia in utter darkness.

She sat on the floor, her leg throbbing, her eyes seeing nothing.

Chapter 2

Mia's eyes dilated in the blackness. Her breathing came out too loud in the sudden darkness that surrounded her, encasing her in a mounting fear. Her leg throbbed, causing her to twitch in pain. She bent down to clutch it, wincing as her fingers gripped at the flesh that had been crushed by the force of the shutting door.

Her heart pounded in her chest, her breath ragged. She could hear herself breathing. She could *hear herself breathing!* She was not used to such silence. She didn't like silence.

No, no, no! It was too quiet. There was no way she was here. She was supposed to be safe outside the wall, and now look where she was. Alone. In the dark. *I have to get out of here.* Her mind whirled. Her pulse pounded in her veins. She didn't know what to do. It was so dark and… *Stop! Stop, stop, stop!*

She took a moment, regathering herself. She could not lose herself. She would not freak out, she would not. It was just blackness. It was just silence. It was just... empty. There were no people. No one was around, and it was dark—so, so dark. The silence pounded against her ears in a way that it never had before. It sent shivers through her. The musty smell that entered her nose brought an uncomfortable saliva to her mouth as she sniffed at the air, trying to figure out if any other human beings were alive in this—this place. She took a hesitant step forward, letting her senses extend, feeling out what may or may not be in the room—or rooms? Her eyebrows drew together, and she breathed out slowly, trying to gain her bearings and understanding of this new place.

She seemed to be inside, yet she sensed doorways, as if there was a place that she could leave but would still be stuck. If she could leave and be stuck at the same time... She must not think of that now. She must get out—but in order to get out, she had to find her way around and figure out where she was. She was in a room. Inside. She knew that for sure. There was the sense of a ceiling over her. She was... sort of surrounded by walls? She sensed walls, yet she sensed doorways opening to more beyond. There was something more to the area that she was in, but she just didn't know quite what it was yet. She blinked, the darkness becoming, well, darker. She put her hand out in front of her face, wiggling her fingers to see if she could even see movement in the darkness. Shaking her head, she let her eyes scour the darkness, as if she could soap it away and bring light.

Hands in front of her, Mia put a foot out slowly, slowly, now knowing if there was a drop off—though she couldn't sense one, or anything *else* that lay beyond. Her heart rate slowed. Problem solving in the midst of chaos, this was what she was good at. Problem solving. She could do this. She closed her eyes, and why not? She was in darkness anyway. She took another step forwards, then another, and another and her hand brushed against a hard surface. She froze. The hard surface was definitely a wall. But what did the wall surround? She couldn't make herself go back into the center of the room. Her breathing became louder, and her eyelids flew open, as if it would help her gather her bearings once again. She slid along the wall slowly. She was used to being sure of her surroundings, of knowing where she was and what to do. But now, in this new world, she did not know what she was supposed to do. She sensed an opening in this strange space, yet at the same time she was within a wall that would not let her go. There was no way out, no way, no… If she kept her head, she would be okay. She knew it: *it will be okay, it will be okay, it will be okay, I just need to keep my head.*

She stopped, took a deep breath, and reached out farther—air. Air. She felt the wall and found a corner, her heart beginning to thump. She stilled herself, ready for anything, everything all at once. There was no telling what would come to her if she ventured into this new place, this new… room? This new world? *Have I been transported into a new dimension?*

She shook her head. She had to keep moving, had to figure out where she was, or she would lose her mind. That was the first step to figuring out where she was in her situation. Her fingers crept around the opening in the wall as a spider's legs would. She slowly, oh so slowly, put her other hand around the corner. *What will I find?* Her heart sped up again, ignoring her thoughts that got faster and faster that she *must, must, must* Stay calm. She had to. Her, well, maybe not her life, but her sanity depended upon it. She could do anything she set her mind to as long as she believed in herself.

Pulling herself inside, she was blinded as lights flared to life all at once. She halted, blinking rapidly as if something had gotten in her eyes. As they adjusted to the light, she saw the room before her had black walls and an open doorway on each wall. *So, I was right. There were more rooms, but doorways also.* She turned in a circle, her bravery slipping from her as sweat dribbles down one's forehead.

She forgot who she was all at once, forgetting what she had just been telling herself. She didn't know where she was—but—but...

"Knock it off!" she yelled, surprising herself so much that she stopped spinning, plopping down on the floor like a toddler would when about to throw a tantrum. She stared in front of her, at the dark doorway ahead of her. It loomed ominously there, just there, in the light. She closed her eyes, back and shoulders stiff just in case someone was creeping up in—not the darkness, the light behind her. Her chest rose and fell. Rose and fell. She breathed in deeply one more time, then exhaled, opening her eyes again. She rose to her feet, walking forward as if she had all the confidence in the world, as if she was not in a strange place that she did not understand. As if she did not—

She got up and walked through the doorway into the next room. The lights flickered on again. She stopped, looking around.

"Welcome home." A female voice filled the room. Mia froze, her eyes darting around, curious, anxious, serious, needing to find out who this person was.

"Who are you? Where are you? When I get my hands on you—"

The voice chuckled. "You are in no place to make threats, my dear."

"Who are you?" Mia growled, her fists clenching.

"I am nobody; nobody you need know. Just know that I am your friend."

"Friend, huh?"

"Yes, friend. I saved you from that wicked world out there, and now you are safe from that tragic world."

"I earned my place in that *'tragic world!'*" Mia said, looking around for the source of the voice. It came from a woman, but she saw no speakers, no technology embedded in the walls.

"Who. Are. You?" she demanded, enunciating every word she spoke, as if the woman had not heard her the first time.

"No need to know, just that I am here to take care of you. You'll be fine here."

"But where am I?" she yelled, raising her voice at last. "Where am I?" There was no response. Mia stamped her foot, folded her arms, and set off looking around the corners, trying to see if there were any signs of technology in the room. She saw none. She walked the whole room, examining the walls, the ceiling, the floor. She knocked on the wall, but it was solid. She went through another door.

Her leg throbbed as she limped through doorway after doorway, hoping in the slightest she would find the exit, someway, any way. If she stumbled upon it, then she might escape. She couldn't just give up. There was no way she was going to let this mysterious person who had taken her away from her new home fool her into thinking that she was safe here. She was not safe here—far from it. She knew not who had taken her. She knew not where her friends were. But she had to escape. She had to see the sun again.

Oh! The sun! How brightly it shone. She remembered the way it shone in the sky, the brightness that blinded her eyes. She remembered the way the blue sky arched above her in one long stretch that seemed to go on forever and ever until it met the city skyline. Now, all she had was the black walls of her imprisonment. She had to get out, to see the sun again, to see the sky, to see her friends! *Where are they? Are they safe? What are they doing? Are they worried?* No. *Why should they be worried? They didn't need to care about her.* She was an independent woman. She could get out of this mess by herself. She had no reason to worry if they were coming for her, for of course she would escape.

She had to get out of here. She would. She just knew it. She had only to be clever enough.

Where did that woman's voice go off to? Mia wondered despite her determination to not be worried about anything. She should not over-obsess about where that voice went.

When she walked into another room, no light turned on to show her which way she ought to go. She stopped, glancing over her shoulder to see the bright light from the room she had just left before facing the blackness ahead. She took a few more steps forwards to see if lights would show her the ways she might go, but nothing happened. Sticking her arms out, she allowed her senses to stretch before her. She ran into no objects. The room was empty. She inched her way forwards, and then suddenly another light blinded her. Another room, one identical to the others. This was a maze. This *had* to be a maze. The room she had just walked through was still black; the room she was now in was bright with light.

14

She hesitated, unsure what to do. If she stepped forward…
what would happen? Anything could happen in this strange place.
She wouldn't allow herself to remain in the same place for long;
if she did, she would be admitting defeat to herself, which was
something that she refused to do. She would not be defeated. *Why
didn't I stay in the room I had originally been put into?* her mind
berated her. *Why was I singled out? Why me? Why now? If it was
going to happen, why not right after I left my last prison, instead
of being promised lifelong safety?* Her mind played with her
thoughts, trying to distract her from her end goal.

Mia walked forward, her eyes alert, ready for anything to
spring at her. She spun in a circle, thinking that she had heard
something, but no. It was all in her imagination. There was
nothing she had to fear - except that she was in this maze place
with no means to get out other than her brains, which were
obviously not working again. She turned her legs right and
walked through another door, halting as the lights did not flick
on. There was some sort of sequence here… but what was it? Did
the lights turn on as an every other room type of thing? She
increased her pace, the pain in her leg causing her to slow, her
mind screaming in protest and urging herself onwards. She must
go - go - go! The next room, the light clicked on. *Is it some sort
of pattern? There has to be some sort of pattern!* Mia stumbled.

"Crud," she grumbled. The pain was such an
inconvenience. Her mind urged her to *run, run, run!* She had to
move faster to figure out the pattern, though she wasn't able to
see all the rooms with the lights on again at once. She had to
walk back through her pattern to figure this out and get to the
exit. She didn't know how big this place was, and she might take

hours to figure out if she had gone through all the rooms. She didn't know how she would manage. But she must try.

She picked up her pace again, her leg throbbing insistently. *Rest, rest, rest,* it seemed to say. *No, no, no,* she responded. Who needed rest? She certainly did not. She would solve this puzzle and escape as fast as she possibly could! She could not afford breaks, not with this weird, mysterious voice that talked to her, that supposedly is a woman who has a body, who told her that she was safe in this space that is obviously not safe. This place was not, *not* safe! Not compared to the outside world. She couldn't *believe* that she was stuck in another horrendous situation. She did not need this. Nobody needed this after what she had been through.

She stopped, her chest heaving in an effort to catch her breath. She considered her options. How was she going to figure out this pattern? Would there be a way for her to figure out how to get out? Was there even a way out that she might possibly find? Would this task be like the 'game' where she spends years and years - maybe forever trying to get out? Her breathing quickened at the thought of remaining here forever, as she had behind The Wall. She couldn't stand that thought. She couldn't be stuck somewhere else after she had just escaped for the rest of her life. She couldn't, couldn't, couldn't! She took a deep breath. She had to focus on getting out of here. She must not freak out.

It began to dawn on her that there would be no way she would find her way out by randomly finding a pattern. Why did she even think that she *might* get out? There was no way she was going to get out. *No, no, I mustn't think like that!* She clenched her fists as she summoned all her strength to get the doubt that had entered her mind. She had to straighten her mind. She was not one to think about what might happen. She didn't need to be the worry wart, the one who came up with all the bad scenarios, like the unlikely hood that she would ever, or would ever escape this place. For there was no way out and— *No!* She could not doubt her ability to escape. She would not give into the little, nasty lies that were skittering through her head.

Her legs moved forwards before her thoughts. She had to find a way out of this. She could not give in to the despair that she crept up in her. But what could possibly happen to show her where she was?

She had to keep moving. As long as she was moving, she felt that she was getting somewhere she hadn't been a moment before. And it was true. The more she moved, the more she would get places. If she stopped, something terrible would happen. If she stopped— "Eli?" She gasped.

Eli was standing right in front of her, his back to her. Eli turned, a grin spreading across his face.

"Mia!" He ran towards her, the light from the room she had just entered glistening on his forehead. "Mia, you're okay!" Mia took a step back, Eli showing all the intent of hugging her. "Eli, how?" She stared at him. He was as real as ever, from the awkward way he stood with most of his weight on his left foot to his curly brown hair that shone unusually bright in the light of the room.

"I found you." His face broad in a smile.

"But how?" She eyed him, uneasiness creeping through her. She crossed her arms. "How in the world did you get in? Did she get you?"

"She? Who she?" Eli asked.

"Who's she?" Mia corrected his grammar, crossing her arms.

"Um… Yeah. Who—whom? —are you talkin' about?" Eli's grin sparkled on his face, as annoying as ever.

"I don't know!" Mia yelled. She gave him a withering look. "I don't know who this person is who ordered me to be taken here. How should I, and more importantly, how do I get out of here? All I care is that I get out! I can't stay here!"

Eli flickered. "Of course you can stay here!" Eli said.

Mia uncrossed her arms. "Excuse me? What's wrong with you?"

"What?" Eli asked, looking like his usual confused self. "How did you get here? Why won't you tell me?" She stared him down. He flickered. *Flickered?* Her eyebrows began creeping up her forehead.

"I—I must have had one too many of Kayla's coffees, huh? My head isn't straight. Now that you mention it, look at this remarkable place!" Eli flung an arm out, looking around, a smile on his face. Mia narrowed her eyes. Something was wrong.

She punched him.

Her fist met no stomach. No grunt of pain, no Eli buckling over. It went right through him. This wasn't Eli. It was an incredibly well made holligram version of him that technology had somehow created. This hologram dupe of Eli was no Eli. How had she even fallen for it?

"You're not even Eli!" she shouted at him, raising her voice despite herself.

18

Eli's—no, the *hologram's* face contorted into one of confusion.

"Mia, what?"

"You're no Eli! How dare you act even stupider than usual?" she asked, anger bubbling up inside her even more than it had before.

"Ouch, how can you even say that to somebody? I'm your friend," the holographic Eli said.

"No, you are *not* somebody. You. Are. A. Fake! I don't like fakes," she snapped, rage bubbling within her.

"You would never, ever dare call me—"

She raised an eyebrow at him. "I just did. You're even dumber as a hologram. I can't believe you fooled me for the slightest bit there." She turned her back on it, staring the way she had come. "You're not even a living being!" She spun back to the hologram of Eli.

"How do you know? And why would you even say that?" Fake Eli looked offended.

"Just leave me alone!" Her voice rose once again as a pang of longing for her friends, her *real* friends, came for her again. "You. Are. A. Fake!" she repeated. She should just give up talking to this fake. Why was she even bothering to talk to him? She puffed her cheeks out. No more. She walked around him, needing to figure out how to get away.

"Where are you going?" fake Eli asked.

"Away from you," she retorted, then chided herself for giving into fake Eli's question. She did not have to explain herself to a non-human.

19

"Why do you want to get away from me?" he persisted, beginning to follow her.

She whirled around, giving him the death glare. "Be gone with you!" she screamed, feeling foolish with the words she had chosen to use.

"What if I don't want to leave you?"

"Then I'll make you go!"

"I don't want to. I want to stay."

"You must go, go! You have no feelings!" she shot back at him. She knew he was an illusion, so why was he even trying to talk to her? Why was she giving into this desperately stupid desire to snap back at a being with no feelings. She continued walking away from the hologram. She would ignore it. And that was final.

Her shoulders stiffened in frustration as she replayed what had happened in her mind. That was a fake. A fake, fake, fake.

"Mia!" The voice was faint. "Mia…" She was not about to look back. She would not look at that hideous hologram that had tricked her so. She couldn't help but notice the hairs on the back of her neck rise up in discomfort, knowing that the hologram's 'eyes' were still following her… following her… following—

"Stop!" she screamed, clamping her hands over her ears. She spun around to find, in the distance, Eli—no, fake Eli—still staring at her. She began walking backwards, slowly at first, but then faster and faster until she slammed against a wall, nearly falling forwards before steadying herself. The pounding in her head was unbearable. She sunk to the floor of the room, clutching her head. Looking up, she was still able to see fake Eli from however far back she had gotten. She shook her head, looking down only to see nothingness. She looked up again, at the alternating rooms of light and darkness. Fake Eli had turned and was staring at her. Beaded sweat moistened her palms. Her breath came out ragged. All at once, fake Eli began moving towards her. She leaped up and blindly ran, smacking into another wall. Shaking it off, she ran as fast as her injured leg could carry her, turning this way and that, faster, then faster, then—

A woman stood in a lit room, but there were no more doorways. Mia skidded to a stop, glancing back to see fake Eli still moving toward her in that eerily determined way of his. She looked back to the woman, trapped.

She was nearly a copy and paste of that woman, Iva, the one who had greeted the group of fighters to the real world. The one who had told them that they were *safe, free.* So much for that.

But this woman was different from Iva. Instead of blond hair swept up into a clean bun, her raven-black hair swooped up into a puffy bun, two strands of hair framing her face. Mascara had been applied thickly, the wings perfectly aligned on either side. She had black eyeshadow, almost as an accident, on her right eyelid, but not on the left. That had been a purposeful, artistic move on this woman's part. The other thing that differed her from Iva, as Mia stared at her, was her black jumper. Not a dress as Iva had worn. But she looked oh so similar. Her neck was long and complemented her long torso in a weird way. Mia blinked.

"Welcome, my child," the woman said. This woman was undoubtedly a fake, like Eli had been a fake. This woman was another hologram! There were no other human people in this wreck of a maze she found herself in. Mia turned her back on the woman, checking fake Eli's progress, but he had halted, standing mid-step, unusually still. She faced the woman again.

"Who are you?" she asked cautiously. She was prepared for this—this *thing* to go crazy again. As the fake Eli had. Her heart thudded in her chest.

"You need not know my name," the woman, robot, hologram, *whatever* said cooly.

Mia shook her head. "I don't know where I am, for one, and for two, that thing - that hologram." Mia pointed behind her, to where fake Eli had probably succeeded in sneaking up behind her, or perhaps was not there at all. "And who are you? You should understand, it would be nice to know at least a little bit about this place, don't you think? If you... If you are real, if you were in my place, how would you feel? You were supposed to be *safe*. To be safe after a *lifetime* of danger and war! What have I done to deserve this? Why am I here? Why me of all the people?" Guilt consumed her. Because *why not her?* "Why did you have to do something like this? At least tell me, please—why am I here?"

"Why wouldn't you be here, my darling?" she asked, her expression softening, almost as a mother would look at her child.

Mia took a step back.

"I don't belong here, and I don't know who you are. Please, tell me."

"Tell you, tell you who I am, my dear." Mia stiffened at the term *dear*. "I am a woman who must remain mysterious."

Mia raised an eyebrow at the woman, judgment radiating from her eyes. She knew the woman could probably see the disgust in Mia's face, but she didn't care. All she cared about was that this woman would not control her life, she couldn't, not after the whole other part of her life had been controlled so horridly.

"Who must remain mysterious," Mia managed to mimic, trying to drip sarcasm but failing miserably.

"It is true. I have brought you to this safe haven, one where no one will ever be able to harm you again!" She raised her arms as if expecting Mia to fall at her feet.

Mia raised an eyebrow. "Well, it seems that the world *you* took me from is the safest place... rather than where I am now, or was, behind..."

The woman's face changed to one of anger. "Well then, Miss. If you are so sure that the place that you left was so brilliant, take a look at this, why don't you?" The woman twitched her wrist and a screen flared to life.

Chapter 3

The screen was as large as one of the black walls,
covering the door to another room. It was like that cinema place
where they showed dramas, though in Mia's opinion the fighting
scenes in the movies were always so faked it was sad.

As she focused on the screen, ignoring the woman, Mia's
eyes widened. A familiar place came to life. Inside the Wall. The
place Mia had grown up.

~

Onto the screen flashed Eli's mother, MaKenzee.. After a
moment, Mia's mother, Martha, appeared, running alongside
MaKenzee. Her long, brown hair that matched Mia's so
beautifully flew behind her as she ran.

"MaKenzee!" There was Eliot, Eli's father, running into
the frame as the camera kept up with the adults.

"Eliot! Watch behind you!" A black man, Harper's father,
roared as he appeared on screen. His face was scratched and
bleeding. A shot from the gun rang out and MaKenzee collapsed,
her eyes bulging, mouth opened in an unuttered scream.

"We need to go," Mia's mother urged.

"I know, I know," MaKenzee said, grinding her teeth. Another gunshot rang out, and MaKenzee's hand clutched her chest. She gasped before her eyes rolled up into her head, and she lay still, unmoving.

A blast of fire drew the attention of whoever was *somehow* filming this event, and Harper's father and Eliot were blown off screen.

"No!" The cry from Mia's mother ripped into the speakers.

"Martha, Martha, we must leave. Help—help me with MaKenzee," Harper's mother was there all at once, the screen latching back onto the three women.

Martha's face showed where the tears had slid.

Martha and Harper's mother bent down, and together they lifted MaKenzee. Men in gold suits rounded a corner. Martha's expression changed to one of fear as she registered their arrival. Gun shots rang out, and Harper's mother collapsed, causing MaKenzee to fall to the ground as she slipped out of Martha's grip. Martha turned, then glanced back at MaKenzee, bending over as if she were about to be sick. She straightened herself up and ran. A man in black pushed through the gold suits, aiming his gun right at Martha, the coldness in his eyes everything. A loud *bang!* rang out, and Martha flopped to the pavement, her eyes staring in great fear at nothing.

~

Mia blinked, attempting to hold back the tears. They streamed down her face anyway, the crying uglier than Mia could

25

ever remember crying. She wiped her nose, sniffling, wishing she could take that stream of tears back as though she had never been crying.

"You see?" The woman's voice brought Mia back to the horrible reality. How was this woman involved in her parent's deaths? She had to be—how else did she have a recording of it?

"What is it I must see?" Mia choked, swallowing hard.

"It is much safer in here."

"*Safer?* Did I just watch my parents die?"

The woman shrugged. "Depends on how you look at things. In a sense, yes; in another sense, you were just watching actors act out the scene."

Mia stared at the woman, not processing what she just had said. "How did you… How did you…" She struggled to understand how the woman had gotten a recording of her parent's deaths. "How? Just how?" She took a step back from the woman, shaking her head in disbelief.

The woman put out her hands out in what Mia recognized as an attempt at a comforting gesture, which did anything but work. This woman would never win her over.

"My dear, it just shows you how horrible the outside world is."

"But that wasn't the outside world!" Mia exclaimed, throwing up her hands in frustration. "Why do you want me?"

"You will grow to understand," the woman crooned, causing Mia's blood to boil.

"I will?" Mia asked skeptically, her eyebrows high, having slightly recovered from watching her parents' deaths.

"You will come to understand when, one by one, all your little friends are here—but they won't be here, because being alone is good. We like being alone. It is the only way to live. To be alone in the dark. The light is harsh on the eyes."

Mia took a few steps back, her fists clenching together, ready, needing to get away from this woman who had done something to her—who had brought her here. She would not let this woman distract her from getting out of here.

"I won't understand. I—I don't want to be here." Mia backed up, preparing to run.

"Running is useless. You can't run from your problems, my dear." The woman took a step towards Mia.

"Don't call me dear," Mia retorted. She turned.

"You can't escape," the woman crooned.

Mia didn't turn back.

"Don't even try," the woman insisted.

Mia began running, frustrated by the limp her injured leg caused.

"You won't ever see the sun again!"

Mia halted, glancing back, trying to mask the emotions that were billowing within her like storm clouds before gushing out all the fury it had been holding in.

~

The wall loomed above her, her hair hanging down her neck. She looked over at Harper, who was scuffing the ground with her foot.

27

"You think we'll ever get out of here?" Mia asked, crossing her arms and contemplating the wall.

Harper shrugged. "I don't know. Seems like something that only a miracle would bring. I don't think we'll be able to… to get to the brick, not after our parents…" Tears sprung to Harper's eyes. "I think it's too dangerous…"

"Well of course it's too dangerous!" Mia snapped. "It's all too dangerous! We are in a life and death situation. If you ever thought it was going to be easy, you were lying to yourself!" she said, flinging her hands up.

A blast from a gun reached the friend's ears. "We need to get out of here," Mia said, grabbing Harper's arm.

"I told you to begin with that this was a bad idea. Gideon would be furious if he knew we snuck out!" Harper blamed Mia faster than Mia could think.

"I know, I know," Mia said, pulling Harper along behind her. Harper's speed sometimes infuriated her. "But I needed to get out." The two stumbled along.

~

A knife was at Mia's throat. She stiffened, sitting straight on the hard cafeteria seat. The clattering of dishes and sound of people talking filled the cafeteria.

Eli stood up, a look of shock plastered upon his ugly face.

"Don't think it's over," a girl's voice growled from behind her.

28

The knife was removed. "Bryn, really?" Mia looked around to see the new companions, Brynlee and Joseph, and their friend Wayde. Joseph had spoken.

"Can't I have some fun?" Brynlee grumbled. "I had to let her go. You know how I feel about that."

"Just stop," Joseph said, his eyes flitting to Harper, who squirmed under his gaze, then back to Brynlee.

Mia stiffened. She didn't like the way boys looked at Harper, like she was something to prey on. Even though Joseph's look wasn't as disturbing as some, she still didn't like it. Boys liked Harper. And in all rights. Harper was gorgeous.

"Wha…" Eli's annoying voice reached Mia's ears, snapping her out of her worries about Harper's life.

"Sorry," Joseph said, looking at Eli. "She hates loose cannons."

Mia wrinkled her nose. "Loose cannons?" she asked, not understanding the reference.

"Sheldon made her let you go," Joseph said, sliding, *uninvited,* into a vacant seat at their table. Mia bristled at the strangers making themselves at home here, of all places. How dare they?

~

The crowd of people bumped into Mia as she made her way to Eli and Bryce. She rolled her eyes to herself as Eli's gaze rested on her for one moment too long. She glared at him, her stomach flip-flopping at the prospect of today. Would today be the day that they actually beat the game? Would they actually win freedom for the rest of their lives? She didn't dare hope. She had to smother the doubts about how many lives they might lose.

"Hey," Eli said, his eyes flitting up and down her body.

"Hi," she said flatly.

"Seen Brynlee and the others yet?" He shifted nervously.

That girl! "Uh, no, and I don't care too."

"Welp, they are on our team..." Eli said, his eyes going behind her. "Hey, there they are!" He pointed.

Mia turned to see the trio of friends walking towards them, parting the crowd just with Brynlee's presence. Her stern look, the knife strapped to her side, and the way she carried herself exuded dominance to everyone else in the room.

Travis and Silvia were not far behind them.

"You ready for this?"

Mia turned to see Harper. She shrugged. "As ready as I'll ever be I guess. It's not like it's any different from our other raids."

"Oh, but it is," Harper said, her eyes moving behind Mia to where Brynlee continued approaching them.

Mia looked over at Eli again, her hatred for him blossoming even more. He seemed to think that she *liked him.* Liked him? That was the stupidest thought he had ever had, and he had had some very stupid thoughts! She couldn't stand him at all! There was no way she would ever like *Eli.*

~

Mia blinked, the memories from behind the Wall erasing as suddenly as they had overtaken her. She touched her cheek, realizing that a tear was sliding down her face. Did she... Did she miss her old life? For now, it seemed like she did.

Chapter 4

You can't run from your emotions, dear, echoed in Mia's head as her legs carried her back through room after room after room. You can't run from your emotions, you can't, you can't, you can't.

Oh, yes, I can, said another voice. The image of her father exploding, being flung off screen, burst into her mind's eye again. She closed her eyes, nearly tripping, trying to escape the oncoming flashes of what she had been shown. She had never had any context on how her parents died. She couldn't seem to stop replaying what she'd seen, she couldn't. It replayed again and again, and again!

You can't run.
Yes, I can.
You can't run from your emotions, dear.
Oh, yes, I can.
Why even try to run?
Why not try to run?
Why run at all? Why not sit and rest in this haven?
Run.
Run.
Run.

Mia's feet pounded the floor, the floor she could see one second but not the next, the floor she disliked the look of but could not look away from.

Why even try to run, my dear?

Mia screamed. A scream of anger. A scream of frustration. But most of all, a scream of regret that she had not been able to spend more of her life with her parents. The parents she would never see again, could never get comfort from again. The parents who would listen to her and—

No! Don't dwell on that! Run, run, run. That's all I can do at this point.

But it wasn't. Mia couldn't keep running. As determined as she was to continue running, her injured leg gave out. She collapsed to the hard ground as the sobs she had buried inside her came wrenching out, one sob at a time.

The tears dampened her face, dripping onto her legs and running down to the floor, demonstrating the mess her life had become. She hated crying.

She knelt on the ground, her left knee digging painfully into the cement. Her life was over. It was over. There was no way she could get it back on track. She would never have a normal life. She would be stuck in here forever—but no. She couldn't let herself think that way. She couldn't. But then—but what if she never escaped?

She had done *something* wrong, and now she was paying the price. Her friends were probably glad to be shot of her anyways. It was her fault she was here, and she began to suspect that maybe she shouldn't bother trying to escape. *Maybe I will be happier here. Maybe my friends will be happier without me. I would be happier without me...*

She looked up, startled at that last thought. She had never thought of that before. What was going on with her? Was she going crazy? What was this place doing to her?

Mia pushed herself to her feet, determined not to let herself down. She got herself into this mess, meaning that she could get herself out. There was a way. She had the will to escape, somewhere, deep down anyways.

She freed her feet, allowing them to wander wherever they wished. Trying to map out the maze hadn't worked, so why should another plan succeed? She would wander, and maybe, maybe she would come across the room she had begun in. But how would she know if she was back in that room? Would she just... know? Probably not. She shook herself, trying to shake out the daunting feeling hovering over her.

"I got this." She said the words that were so cheesy out loud. She was okay with using those words 'you got this' for someone else, but to herself, no. Too silly, too weak. Too... childish.

She would be her own leader in this time of crisis—and this was undeniably a crisis. She had to lead herself out. She would. She simply had to keep her head and do as she always did. Her best. If she could remain in control of her emotions and go for it, all in, she would escape. There was nothing that would get in her way! Nothing right now, anyway.

That woman—the woman who had shown her the gruesome ways her parents and her friends' parents had died—was another mystery she must solve. Why did this woman want her here? Why did this woman show her parents' deaths? How could someone be so cruel as to show someone their loved one's death? There had to be an answer to these questions. She would not allow them to go unanswered.

Chapter 5

"**You** know, this place is a wonderful place to live. Here, alone, in the dark."

The woman's voice shattered the glass of Mia's thoughts just as she had finally gained control of her thoughts and emotions. Mia whirled in a circle, trying to find the woman's voice. "There is no one to answer to here. No one to tell what to do. No one to order around. It's just you, yourself, and I."

"And, who is the *I* in this situation?" Mia asked, looking up at the ceiling but seeing no speakers to account for the source of the voice. Nothing indicated human life other than herself and the light that shone into the room she inhabited.

"I, my friend"—Mia bristled at the implication that her captor could be her *friend*—"prefer to remain mysterious." *Mysterious!* Mia snorted. She couldn't believe this woman.

Mia decided that the best course of action was to ignore this woman. Ignore her and hope that she vanished into whatever weird place that this woman came from.

"I see you have found a place to sleep?"

Mia's eyebrows raised in amusement despite her determination to ignore the voice. She had not the slightest wish to sleep.

"This would be such a nice place to make yourself at home, don't you agree?"

Mia couldn't agree less. A black box, with four doors leading to nowhere? She could think of a million other places that she would rather live. She would not let this woman force her into thinking this was a reasonable place. This was no holiday. There was no convincing her that this was a good place to stay— this was, in all reason, a nightmare unfolding.

"This room that you are in will help you to feel comfortable." The voice went on as if giving Mia an orientation tour. "Here, you will sleep well and eat well. This will be the room you most enjoy, as you have chosen to stay here, in this room, the longest."

This woman was something else. Mia began moving, determined to get out of this place.

"No, don't leave this room yet. You have not heard all the benefits of it!" the woman cried out. Mia ignored her. She didn't need to listen to this fake woman. "It's never too hot or too cold," she went on as Mia walked into the next room. This was a dark one, one where she could not see her feet as she walked in the general direction of the next door right in front of her.

"No! Go back!" The voice echoed in her ears.

Mia quickened her limping steps. If she was upsetting the woman, maybe this was the right direction to go in. She continued limping along, her smashed leg throbbing more painfully than ever. She had to get it checked. Where was Norah when you needed her? Norah was Eli's brother's wife. The two had just gotten married and were now off on their honeymoon, as far from New Jersey as they could get. Mia couldn't blame them.

Norah's blessing was to heal the hurt and injured, something that would be useful at the moment.

"That room you just left will be your safe space," the voice continued. "You will go back to it continually, because it is the safest room in the maze."

Mia halted, her eyebrows pulling together.

Had that woman just told her that that was 'the safest' room in the maze? This did not bode well… What may happen if she left her safe—

No! Nowhere in this place is safe! This place is far from safe!

She frowned, concentrating on what the woman had said. Maybe this place could be a safe place. Maybe, just maybe—but no. Why would she have been taken from the outside world? Why just her? Where were her friends, what were they doing? If this place was supposed to be safe, then her friends ought to be here too. This place was far from safe.

Mia shook herself. She had to ignore the words that the woman was dripping into her mind. She had to pick up her pace and learn to move on to her way of escape. Mia moved her legs, taking her to a dark room. The darkness encompassed her eyes and gave them a hug, giving her a moment of relief from her momentary panic. She allowed her eyes to focus on the darkness, her mind slowly relaxing. Mia's leg throbbed. *Did she really need to keep going? Was running still the best option? What if she just found a room to relax in?* Her stomach gurgled.

If they really provided her food, she would never have to worry about how or where she would get food. If she stayed here, she would be safe from any unknown territory—though this whole palace was an unknown territory. She turned to her left and continued on. The outside world had brought dangers that she had slowly been learning about, like that one time Brynlee put her knife to Mia's throat as a joke in that diner and everyone freaked out. The men in suits came who had weapons and asked lots of questions, eyeing Brynlee like she was a psychopath even though it had been a joke. It reminded her of Behind The Wall, giving her flashbacks, flashbacks she had never wanted to repeat, flashbacks that scared her more than anything.

Maybe, just maybe, being surrounded by a black box was the safest place to be. She rather liked the dark, she admitted to herself as she took a step in the general direction of the door. Maybe she could live here. There might be the chance that she would grow to like it, learn to be content where she was. If she learned to like it here, she might never need to worry again. Yes! That was it! She would settle in here and be a loner. She seemed to do best on her own anyway. She didn't need to worry about anyone else, she didn't need to concern herself with people who did not like her—or liked her too much. Yes. That would be her plan. She would settle in here for a long, lovely life, one full of contentment and no worries.

Mia sat down in the middle of the black room. She sat, and she sat. Her throbbing leg pulsed with pain, so she lay down on the floor, releasing the tension she had been holding for who knew how long. The sunlight she had been in hours ago seemed like a faint memory. Or was it all in her imagination?

Yes. She had imagined the sun, she had imagined there was an outside world, she had imagined the friends she grew up with. She had no friends after all, no real friends who cared about her. She was content to be on her own, and maybe that was how it should be. There seemed to be something, though… Something that rather reminded her of a bright light and nearly blinded her if she looked at it for too long. It shone in the dark and went down at night before dozens of mini versions of it twinkled in the—

She gasped, sitting up so fast the blood rushed to her head. She had seen something! Something like that bright thing that shone in… In where? The image she thought she had seen disappeared as quickly as it popped into her mind. She laid back, disappointment sweeping through her. The moment her head hit the ground, she forgot what she thought she had remembered. That sun was no more. She was no more. She didn't know what she had been thinking. She probably made it up after all.

She stared at the black ceiling, the ceiling she couldn't see through the blackness. It was too black, too black, too—

Her eyes slid shut. The temperature was just right, giving her good reason to want to stay there for a longer period of time. She had been moving for such a long time, such a long time indeed.

~

She didn't know how long she lay there. She didn't know if she fell asleep. All she knew was, all at once, she was staring into blackness again, something sorrowful seeping through her. She couldn't quite identify what it was she was feeling deep inside her gut. She had something… But…

She scratched at an itch on her arm. It had never itched there before. Strange. She sat up, still staring into the blackness of the room, her mind wandering from fuzzy memory to fuzzy memory, unsure of what she had done or what she would do in the future. It really didn't matter, anyway. She would be here forever, and that was alright.

A slight disturbance caused her to shift. She heard a strange noise, one she had not heard in she didn't know how long. But then it was gone, and she figured it was just the workings of the inside of her new home. Of the place that she could now feel comfortable in and not worry about anything attacking her. She was safe here. No one to bother her, no one to—

There it was again. Someone's breathing. Who was there? *No one. That is who.* There were no people in this maze but her; her senses told her so.

"Mia?"

This was a place of silence. No birdsong filled the air, no rustling of trees. For once in her life she could have complete silence, something that she had never heard before. This complete silence was... mesmerizing.

She walked over to a corner and pressed herself in it.

"Mia?"

There was no such thing as other people in this world. There could not be a person talking. *No, no, no!* She had to get her head back on track. Her mind played tricks on her all the time. She could sit here and never need to eat. She could sit here and never need to sleep. Darkness brought her calmness. Darkness brought her peace.

"Mia! Where are you?"

Mia covered her ears. She was playing. Her brain was doing something to her, and she didn't know what she needed to do. Her mind was talking to her. She needed to clear her mind and forget the things that were not here.

She shook her head.

Clear your head, girl. She had to get it out of her head that someone was looking for her, for no one would look for her. Why would someone go look for her? No one cared for her. No one at all, and this was just the way of things. No one wanted to be friends with her. Her mind repeated again, and again, and again.

"Mia! Oh, Mia, where are you?"

Mia's head snapped up. Harper. That was Harper's voice.

Chapter 6

"**Mia!** Mia! You're here, I knew it!" Mia stood up so quickly her head spun. That was Harper's voice. Harper, her friend, her *real* friend. She knew she had a friend. There was someone who cared for her; she wasn't alone in this world. Her friend had come to save her! Her friend was here, she was here! Harper was here, here, here!

Mia took a shaky step forward, having been cramped in a small position for so long.

"Harper?" Her heartbeat sped up, and a bead of sweat ran down her forehead. "Harper!" She began to limp in the direction she thought she heard Harper's voice. No thought crossed her mind of the fake Eli she encountered earlier. No doubt, this was the real Harper. It had to be, no matter how unlikely it may be after the fiasco with fake Eli.

"Mia!" Harper's voice was louder. Mia broke into a slow, limping run.

"Harper!" Mia's eyes strained as she limped through room after room, trying to find her friend. "Harper! Is that you? Is it really you?"

"Mia!"

Finally, *finally,* Mia ran into a room where the light snapped on and revealed Harper. Her dark, slightly curly hair shone in the brightness.

Harper turned. "Mia!" They ran toward each other, Mia flinging her arms out in a very unMia-like way. She never gave exuberant hugs.

"Oh, Harper, I never—" Mia cut herself off as her arms did not stop around Harper's firm body. Her arms went right *through* Harper, and Mia found she was giving herself a large hug. She stumbled back, staring at Harper, her eyes wide, disbelieving, not wanting to believe what she saw right in front of her face. This was no Harper.

"Mia!" A tear slid down Harper's face.

Harper didn't cry. Hang on, no, that's a lie. She either didn't cry or cried bucketloads, no in between. "You're not Harper. I should have known!" Mia yelled. "Just the same as Eli!" She stomped her foot in childish frustration. "I should have known you are not real, especially so soon after Eli."

"Eli what? You've seen him? He's been missing too. We are all worried sick about him."

About him, not about you, you selfish—

"Eli nothing. Who cares? You go away and stop bothering me!"

"Mia." Harper looked hurt. "Mia, I came to rescue you."

"You did no such thing." Mia snarled at the illusion. "You're an illusion, and I will not heed to your words."

"Heed? When did you become such an eloquent speaker?"

44

"Since when did you begin using words such as eloquent?" Mia asked the illusion, raising her eyebrows at the fake.

Mia's heart twisted inside, yelping to get out. Maybe everything in this place was fake. Maybe everything that she had ever known... What if the outside world never existed in the first place? Her stomach churned in fear. Maybe everything had been an illusion... Maybe... The only place that had ever been real was Behind The Wall? Maybe it was all one of those movie shows, and that's how her made up parents had been caught on film... Yes. That would make so much more sense. She had been living in one of those virtual reality things. That made so much more sense to her. The way that—

The spot on her arm itched again. She scratched it.

"Mia?" Harper's illusive voice came to her again.

"Wha—no." Mia stopped herself from acknowledging the silly little thing that was *not* Harper. She would not give in.

"Where are you going?" fake Harper asked.

Mia walked on. She would not speak to it.

"Where are you going?" A hand on Mia's shoulder caused Mia to swing around, looking furiously into Harper's fake eyes. How did Harper have such a firm grip, though she was an illusion? She was not real. She was an illusion. She was not real!

"You are not real, H-Harper," Mia stuttered. Yet she had *felt Harper's hand!* She had felt it! But no way was this Harper. It was like—

"Mia?" Mia whirled around at the sound. It was Eli! No, it was fake Eli! It was the illusion again!

Mia covered her face with her hands, squeezing her eyes shut, trying with all her might to block out the voices.

"Mia?" Eli.

"Mia?" Harper.

"Mia, can you hear me?" Eli.

Mia opened her eyes to see Eli offensively close to her, even by his standards.

Mia stepped back so that the two friends stared into each other's eyes for one heartbeat. They turned to stare at Mia.

"Mia," Eli said, taking a step forward. His eyes were so deep. "Mia, we miss you." His body lurched forwards, his middle glitching like an old TV.

Mia blinked. No. Her friends didn't miss her. This was the fake Eli, and that was the fake Harper.

"Go!" Mia yelled at him "Go! Both of you, you ain't real! You are not a thing!"

"Mia, how could you?" Eli asked, his voice dripping with hurt.

"Because you are *fake! My life's a fake life! I'm not even a real person!"* She halted, never having thought of that before.

Was she even real? She had to think about it. She had a running skill that no normal human in this outside world seemed to have. All of her friends had skills that others she saw in the outside world did not. How was it that she could do this, but no one else seemed to? She had seen runners on television, but the fact that they talked of practicing their whole lives was unrelatable to her. She had always been able to run, with or without practice.

"I am not fake. I am here, standing before you. I am as real as ever." Eli said.

Mia shook her head, refusing to believe. Her whole life had *not* been faked. "No, no, you are fake! I saw you glitch! You are a technology of some sort that I do not understand at all! At all!"

"I am real," Harper added, stepping up next to Eli. "I am real."

Mia looked from one to the other, shaking her head.

"I'm done here." She turned and limped away.

"You can't run away from us, Mia," Harper called after her.

"We are always watching, Mia!" Eli said. "And I can't get you out of my mind!"

Mia broke into an uncomfortable jog.

Chapter 7

"**Harper!**" Mia called. Harper turned, a smile spreading upon her face.

"Hey, what's up Mia?" Harper asked, waiting for Mia to catch up with her. The two walked side by side, Mia's insides filling up with the joy she felt when she was with her best friends. It was a joy that was hard to describe, but she just knew when it was there.

"Have you heard if we are going on a raid soon?" Harper asked. Mia was a group leader in their League, meaning Gideon, their League's leader, sent messages through her when her group was to lead a raid for The Golden Brick, the only hope they had to get out of this prison.

"Nope, not yet," Mia said, brushing some hair out of her eyes.

"Eli's getting restless."

Mia bristled at Eli's name. "What are you getting at?"

"Just that he mentioned he wants to get out there is all. Bryce agrees."

"Well." Mia huffed, crossing her arms. "I guess whatever *Eli* says is always the right thing."

"Mia, why do you always have to be so annoyed at him?"

"Why is he always pranking me?" she asked, turning to Harper.

"Why is who always pranking you?"

Mia peered over her shoulder to see Bryce appearing through a doorway the two had just passed. Mia glanced at Harper, seeing her cheeks turning pink.

"No one you need to know."

"Don't worry, he knows who," Harper said, waving it off.

"Who we talkin' bout?" Eli burst from the room, shoving his way past Bryce. He grinned at Mia, his white teeth gleaming in the fluorescent light of the hallway.

"Oh, some annoying pest," Mia said, staring right at him.

"Well, I just heard from Gideon—" Eli began.

"Of course Gideon tells *you* things!" Mia interrupted, an unexpected fury boiling over all at once. She hadn't anticipated her annoyance at Eli to go over the top. The past few weeks he hadn't done anything to her. But it had only been a few weeks; he always sprung things on her when she least expected it, and it drove her crazy.

Eli stared at her. "Um, yeah, he's kinda my brother..." He trailed off before grinning his obnoxious grin.

"Well, good for you!" Mia snapped.

"Mia," Harper reproved, stepping forwards.

"He's always bragging about himself," Mia snapped, turning to Harper as if Eli wasn't there.

"Um, guys?" Bryce's voice came.

"Mia, that's no reason to—"

"Guys!" Bryce raised his voice. The two girls looked at him.

49

"Gideon is sending us on a raid," Eli said.

Mia's insides broiled. "And he tells *you* this?"

"It was an emergency decision," Eli said, putting up his hands.

"How about we just go and meet Gideon?" Bryce said, seeming to shrink inside himself at the two people arguing.

"Bryce is right. Knock it off, you two," Harper butted in.

Mia stopped. She didn't want Harper angry at her. No one wanted to see an angry or upset Harper. When she got upset, she got *upset*.

"Okay then." Mia shot Eli one more glare. "Let's go," she said, looking at Harper and Bryce, not Eli.

~

Mia continued on her way, her injured leg protesting with all its might against her quick pace. She needed to get away from the fake images of, well, of just one of her friends. Eli, well, she didn't need to think of Eli. Nohe wasn't a friend.

"How's your new life?" The woman stood before her, somehow having appeared without a sound.

"Why would you ask me that?" Mia asked, standing in place and watching the woman with narrowed eyes.

"Because I care for you," the woman said.

"Fat chance." Mia snorted. "How ever could you care for me?"

The woman looked offended. "Why would I not? I am not some evil crook."

"You could prove me wrong. How do I know that you are not some form of technology too? Like Eli and Harper—" She broke off, Harper's smiling face flashing before her eyes and twisting her heart.

The woman smiled a thin, wicked smile. "My dear."

Mia twitched with irritation. "Don't call me that."

"Okay. Mia, this is your real life. You have always—"

"No, this is not my life. You are wrong!" Mia snapped, interrupting the woman, or the figure, or whatever.

"How could I possibly be wrong?"

"Because you are… You know what?" Her voice rose. "I'm done." She stormed away as fast as her legs would carry her.

"Mia." Harper's voice.

Mia ignored it. There was no way she would fall for anything this maze had in store for her again. She had fallen for the maze's tactics too many times already.

"Who knows where Mia is, Eli," Harper's voice came again.

Mia kept on going.

"But Harper, we can't just not follow someone we heard talking about her! How can we not follow a lead that we have?" Eli's voice. Mia's walk slowed.

"Well, we can't be stupid either, Eli!"

"Wow, thanks Harper."

Mia found herself fixating on the voices and stopped walking.

"I'm going after them." Eli.

"No, you are not." Harper.

"Yes, I am." Eli. "I'm not letting a lead on Mia get away. I'm going!"

"Eli, wait!"

"I won't!"

"Oh, Eli." Harper.

Mia blinked. She was back in the room, alone. What had happened? Had there been some sort of glitch in the system of this room? Had it tried to trick her again somehow? She shook her head, walking again. The voices continued as she entered room after room.

"Eli, wait."

"Harper, don't let me get caught."

"Well, don't be an idiot and go by yourself!"

"Where's Maria?"

"She went to get more help."

"A lot of good it'll do now that we have a lead and the others don't know."

"I knew we should have gotten one of those flat things the others carry around to communicate with people." "Those things are useless." Static.

Then, so loud Mia flinched.

"Stop, they are going to see you." Harper again. "It's fine, Eli. I just don't want you getting—"

"Excuse me!"

"Eli, no! Don't talk to them!"

"No, but they may know where Mia is—"

"Hush!"

A deep, scary voice butted in. "Did you say Mia?"

"Yes and—"

"Hush!"

Mia needed to keep walking, to ignore the voices, the fake voices. This was all made up. Her life was all made up.

"E—I mean, it does not matter, it was a mistake. He, Elijah, is not in his right mind," Harper's voice said.

"Is that so, well."

The sound cut off, leaving Mia in silence. Nothing to hear, nothing to see, for she stood in a dark room. It took her a moment to realize a tear was sliding down her face. The voices of those whom she thought were her friends were gone. She didn't know if she would ever hear Harper's voice again. She didn't know what would happen next, but it may not be good. It may be okay, but it might not be. Something always went wrong when she was not here, after all, right? Right? If there was a place she could be safe, it must be this maze. This must be the palace that would bring her safety and comfort, joy and happiness. Her friends would never come and save her. *Save me? Why would they need to save me?*

Though she had heard their voices, she knew it was just voices in her head. There was no way anybody would come looking for her. Why would anyone come looking for her? She was just a simple, boring person with no personality.

"Eli, would you stop?" Harper.

"No, I won't stop." Eli.

"Eli, what if we get caught? What if we—" Harper's voice squeaked in surprise.

A rough voice sounded in the dark room Mia had limped into. "You kids seem to be following us. What's the deal?"

"We're mistaken. He thought you looked like somebody else. Come on, Elijah."

"You know, I feel like I've heard that name before," another man's voice said.

"Me too, it's very familiar."

"We're nobody," Harper's voice assured. "We'll just get out of your way. Sorry about El-Elijah."

"I don't think you need to go anywhere," the first man's voice said.

"But, but we just made a mistake," Harper said, her voice shaking.

"Exactly," a man said. "That's why you should come for a visit."

"A... visit?" Harper stuttered. "Um, no, I think—"

"I think so," the second man's voice said. "You're Harper, right?"

"How do you...? Elijah, let's g—"

"Oh, I don't think you'll be going anywhere, darlin'," the second voice said. Mia stared into the darkness, not liking the sound of what was happening in this simulated world.

"Hey, Elijah—oomph!" A thudding sound.

"Har—" Eli's voice stopped mid sentence.

"Get off me!" Mia looked up towards where the ceiling should be.

"Harper!" Mia called, forgetting, for the moment, that she was in a room all by herself, without anyone. Her mind flashed to Eli and Harper, who were struggling.

But then, she was alone, and her friends were not real. She had made them all up. She was imagining all the visuals that would have come with the voices of her friends.

"Get off!"

"No."

"Eli!"

"Who?"

"Shush!"

"Put me down!"

"Stop!" Mia bellowed.

The voices snapped off. Silence filled the room.

Mia stood there.

And stood there.

And stood there.

Her breathing came out loud and irritating. She winced, the sound annoying to her own ears.

She held her breath for three, two, one, then let it out in a sigh that caused her fingers to curl up. She couldn't stand this silence!

Silence was awful! Yet it was necessary.

This room, like all the rooms that connected room after room, was her new home. She lived, loved, and ate here. She had so much to live for here. Herself. That was enough. She never need answer to anyone here. She could live for herself and didn't need to worry about people. Who needed people? That random woman who talked to her was unimportant, but it was nice to know she had a person she could talk to if she needed.

She plopped down in a lit room, sitting and enjoying the silence. She closed her eyes, inhaling as if a warm summer's afternoon wind-breeze blew in her face.

A memory crept up into her mind, one that filled her to the brim, no matter how fictional it may have been.

~

"Mia, dear," her mother called from the room she shared with her parents. Mia was there in an instant, jumping onto her parent's bed and giving her mother a side hug.

"Don't forget, we are about to leave for a raid," her father informed her, sitting on the other side of her. He put an arm around her, dropping a kiss on her forehead. "We love you, you know that, right Mia?"

Mia snuggled into his side. "Yes, Daddy, I do." She closed her eyes.

"Why don't you run along and find Harper?" her mother asked, standing up. "We are due to meet her parents, along with Travis' and Eli's parents, in a few minutes."

Mia wrinkled her nose at Eli's name.

"Now, don't you go and get into fights with him, you hear?"

"He's the one who always starts the fights!" Mia protested.

Her mother gave her a loving look. "Even so, behave yourself, my child. You are a strong girl, and we'll see you soon, I promise."

56

Mia got up reluctantly, walking to the door of the room. She paused, looking back at her parents, both smiling at her as she left the room.

~

Harper trailed along behind Mia as she walked briskly towards Gideon's chamber, the place where Eli's brother lived. His circular room was the most unique room in the whole base. He rarely left, but for the few team meetings he'd held so far.

"What do you think Gideon wants?" Harper puffed, struggling to keep up with Mia's pace.

"Probably to send us on a raid," Mia said, not slowing down for Harper. Compared to Mia, everybody walked slowly, no matter how slowly she went.

She entered the room, letting her steps slow. Harper caught up, looking towards where Gideon stood by his 'throne chair' in the middle of the room, staring at the door. He gave a slight nod as Mia and Harper entered the room.

"Just waiting for Eli and Bryce now," Gideon said.

"Him?" Mia blurted.

"Yes. That *him,* lady, happens to be my brother," Gideon said, glowering at her.

Gideon always has an attitude, Mia thought with an attitude of her own. She kept it to herself, though, refusing to allow her annoyance to show.

"Well, I guess you are right," she snapped, rolling her eyes at Harper.

Harper raised her eyebrows at Mia. "Mia, really, today of all days?"

"Of all days? What does that even mean?" Mia snapped.

"The day our parents went on a raid all together!" Harper said, giving a playful eyeroll.

"I'll beat you to the room!" Eli's bratty voice came from the hallway.

"Oh!" Mia huffed, throwing her hands up in frustration.

"I'm too lazy to run," Bryce said. He was almost worse than Eli.

Of course Bryce was too lazy to run. He was *always lazy.*

"Heyyyyy brother!" Eli shouted as he entered the room, spreading his arms out wide, a stupid grin on his face.

"Hey Harp," Eli said, waving like a maniac to Harper. She gave a small smile.

"Hey, Miaaaaa!" Eli called. Mia turned to face Gideon as the boys came to stand next to Harper.

"Wassup bro?" Eli asked Gideon.

Gideon pursed his lips. "If you would let me speak, brother," Gideon said, giving Eli a cold stare, "I might be able to tell you the news."

"We're going on our own raid, and we are going to win!" Eli pumped his fist in the air.

"Don't get ahead of yourself, bud," Mia said.

"Well, it's okay to hope, ain't it?" Eli said.

"Don't say ain't!" Mia retorted.

"Now, now," Gideon said. "If you don't quit squabbling, then I won't be able to tell you the news!"

"The what?" Eli asked, a stupid grin on his face.

"The news!" Gideon roared. "For gosh brother, can't you behave yourself for one moment?" He rolled his eyes.

"Okay, geeze, I—" Eli held up his hands.

"Nevermind," Gideon said, interrupting Eli. "Nevermind, nevermind. I'll just make the announcement myself." He looked around the group of people. "All your parents were on a raid together, yes?"

Everyone nodded, agreeing. "So we get to go on one together now, right?" Eli asked, bouncing on the balls of his feet.

Gideon shot him a look. "This is not about you. Well, it kind of is, but you make this so difficult!" He tugged at his hair, seeming to have lost control for a moment, then took a deep breath. Gideon looked at the people before him. He looked at each person one at a time, a long, hard look.

"Hey, where's Travis?" Harper asked. "His parents were with our parents, no?"

"He is on a raid right now too," Gideon responded.

"Course he is," Bryce mumbled. "He always gets to go on more raids than we do."

"Soo…" Eli began, stopping as his brother's eyes shot towards him. "What's the news?" Eli shrugged his shoulders.

The silence in the room seemed to stretch for longer than it should have.

"Our parents…" Gideon's voice caught. He swallowed, staring at the wall above the group's heads.

"Our parents… what? Died? Yeah, good joke!" Eli said, chortling for his own amusement. *He thinks he is so funny.* Mia twitched in annoyance at this person who couldn't take *anything* seriously.

Gideon closed his eyes, squinting his eyes shut as if he could barely stand his brother. Mia could certainly never stand him.

"Yes."

"What?" Eli asked, looking from Mia, to see her reaction to his joke, back to his brother.

"Yes. Our parents are indeed dead."

"Nice one." Eli gave an uneasy laugh as if not fully sure he believed what his brother was saying. He shoved his hands into his pockets. "You're going to have to work a lot harder to get me to believe that!"

Mia's world swayed. Gideon never joked around. Mia shook her head. "No."

"Our parents died on the raid," Gideon repeated himself.

"What?" Eli asked again, his face falling.

"Do you not have ears, brother?" Gideon asked, his face scrunching in frustration.

"Oh, what a thing to joke about," Mia snapped. She turned to face Eli. "Our parents are dead, haha, what a laugh to call everyone here for a prank! A prank, Eli!" Her voice rose in her throat.

"A-are they actually?" A tear slid out of Harper's eye.

Gideon nodded. Mia stared first at him, then at his brother.

"Yes," Gideon said, crossing his arms and looking sternly at the group.

"Oh," Harper gasped. She took a step back, shaking her head.

"I thought it would be best to tell you all together instead of separately."

"Mom and Dad can't be dead," Eli said, staring at his brother in astonishment. "This is one big prank."

"Not everything is a prank, brother!" Gideon raised his voice. "Our parents"—he took a step towards Eli—"are dead! How hard is that to comprehend?"

"Gideo—"

"This is not a game, brother, this is real life. People die here, and that's the way it is. Why would I make a joke out of it?" He stared at Eli before turning and leaving.

Mia stood there in shock, while Eli and Bryce turned to leave. Her mind churned over the information they'd been given. She never imagined what she would do if her parents... No. It couldn't be. They were not dead.

"They..." Mia's voice failed her. "They can't be d..."

"They're dead?" Harper turned to look at Mia, the babbling voices of Eli and Bryce growing fainter, as if nothing had ever happened. As if no one had died. As if it was a normal day. How dare they not even *care* that their parents were gone? It was not right.

"They don't even care!" Mia blustered, swiping at her eyes. She didn't understand how anyone could take that news so cooly.

She began walking, her body stiff as she moved out of the room. She would never understand Bryce and Eli's easy understanding of the news.

~

Mia blinked to find herself back in the room. The memories had come back so... so vividly it had felt real. She shifted in her spot on the floor. The empty room now felt even more empty. Though she knew her previous life was a fake... she... she didn't know what to do. She didn't know how to comprehend that what she thought was her life was, in fact, not.

And her friends... her friends who were not her friends... they were all... all what? They had certainly felt real, appeared more real than any simulations could have possibly made them. There was no way her friends had all been a figment of her imagination. Could it have possibly been her own self making it all up? She gasped, tears welling in her eyes. Determined not to let the tears fall down her face, she blinked them away. She was not a crier. She took the blows of life with little less than a twitch of annoyance. She needed no comfort. She needed no peace. She had it all right here. She had the place she always needed. There were no friends looking for her. There were no enemies against her. All was well.

But then she heard something that sent shivers down her back.

Chapter 8

"Get off!"

Mia's head jerked to attention.

Just another bot.

"Harper, are you okay?" Eli's voice asked, closer than ever.

"Do we look okay?"

"Ah, no," Eli's voice came. It was as if she had never departed from her friends. Man, she must be hallucinating very well now. If she could hear her friends'—*no,* her fake friends' voices so well at the moment that—

"We've got to find Mia."

Mia snorted. She really was going crazy at this point.

"Where are we?" Eli asked

"Um, in a building, obviously. That's where the men brought us. The men *you decided to follow Eli!"* Harper's voice rose to a shriek.

"Okay, okay! I was so stupid, I admit it now!" came Eli's reply.

"Oh, so you admit it *now."* Harper's voice slashed through the air.

"By the way, where do you think Kayla is?" Eli tried to deflect.

A brief image of Kayla enthusiastically handing out energy drinks flashed before her.

"I don't know. I hope she's okay," Harper's voice said.

"Maybe she's with Joseph and Brynlee."

"She said something about going back to the house for something, but I don't know what." Harper's voice explained.

"We don't have time to worry about her right now. Maybe Mia is here." Mia's ears perked up despite knowing this was all probably some large hallucination she had made up.

"Mia!" Harper's voice tugged at her heart.

"Mia! You here?" Eli's followed. She had no wish to go to Eli's voice, but Harper's seemed to tug at her heart. "Mia! Are you here?" That did it.

"Mia!" Harper's voice was full of fright.

Mia took a deep breath. "Harper!" she screamed, her volume hurting her throat.

"Eli!" Harper's voice echoed.

"Harper!" Mia screamed.

"Eli! I heard Mia! She's here!"

"Mia!" Eli's voice called. She glued her lips together, refusing to speak to him.

"Harper!"

"Mia!"

Mia was running now, her hair flipping behind her as she tried to find where Harper's voice came from. She needed to find her, for she was here. Mia knew it. Harper was not a figment of her imagination. Mia could not let that happen. She couldn't.

"Mia!"

64

"Harp—" Mia ran into something.

"Oomph!"

"Harper, you okay—Mia!"

Mia stared at Harper's body on the ground, the body she had accidentally bumped into.

"Harper!" She helped Harper up, pulling her friend into an embrace before stepping back to look her up and down. Harper had a cut over her eyebrow, but other than that, she was unscathed.

"Harper, you're not... you're not an illusion, are you?"

Harper's eyebrows drew together. "Mia, what?"

Mia took a step back, shaking her head. "You're not real. I'm going insane. I'm not falling for this again."

"Again?"

"Mia, what happened to you?" Eli asked, stepping toward Mia.

Mia shook her head again, pulling her arms in to hug her body, trying to become smaller.

"Mia, it's going to be okay. We will get out of here." Mia didn't respond.

"Mia?" Harper asked. "You there?" Harper shifted her weight.

Mia turned and began walking back from the way she came.

"Mia! Mia, come back. We're here to get you out of here! What's gotten into you?" Harper's hand grabbed her shoulder. She wrenched out of the grasp, continuing to walk.

"Mia." Harper. "Mia, come on. Talk to us."

Mia turned around, not wanting to talk to either of her fake imaginings. She stared at Harper, ignoring Eli's lengthy body behind Harper.

"Mia. Please, tell me you're okay. You all right? But you're limping, and everything that just happened can't be that fun for you, and—"

Mia held up her hand. She shook her head, shrugging her shoulders, looking down to avoid Harper's electronic eyes.

"Mia. Talk to—"

"Mia, tell us you're okay, please." Eli's voice slipped over Harper's in that way that crawled around and ate it up.

"Mia."

"Mia."

"Mia."

Her friend's voices bantered around her head, causing her to clutch her ears, trying to block them out because they were all fake, fake, fake! Everything she had known and does know now is fake! There was nothing for her in this dump. She did not need to know anything going on in that world she had made up. Now she was hallucinating so badly that she thought her friends were in this, this *place* with her! She didn't know what... how to get rid of these exhausting visions she was being encompassed in. She shook her head, clutching it harder.

Harper's soft hand on her wrist caused her to look up. Her *firm* hand. Her *firm* grip. Not a robotic figure. Not an illusion that she made up.

"Mia," Harper said, her voice soft. "Mia, are you okay?"

"No." Her voice was barely audible. "No, I'm not." Her knees gave out and Mia was on the floor.

"Mia." Harper sank down next to her. "Mia, what did you go through?"

Tears pricked the corners of her eyes. She bit her lip, looking up, blinking hard. She would not let the tears fall. She would not, not, not let the tears fall! Not in front of Eli.

"You're real?" she whispered.

"What?" Harper asked.

"You're real?" Mia asked, looking Harper in the eyes.

"Of course we are real," Harper said, giving Mia a curious look. "Mia, why on earth would you think we are not real?"

"No reason," Mia said, rubbing her eyes hard with her palms, attempting to get the stupid tears back inside of her, refusing to let them fall.

"Mia, come on. Tell us. It's okay, we're here now. You can tell me what happened."

"What about—"

"Eli, not now." Harper's tone towards Eli gave Mia a smug feeling. Her emotions intertwined, smearing into a dirty tornado, and she couldn't help but feel satisfied that Harper had snapped at Eli. "Mia, please talk to me and tell me what's wrong."

"Everything," Mia muttered, avoiding eye contact once again with Harper.

"Everything? Yeah, I can understand that." Harper's hand went to Mia's chin, forcing Mia to look at her gently. "Mia, you matter. You know that, right?"

Mia jerked out of Harper's gentle grip. "No," she said, needing to get out of here and back to herself. "No, I don't. You should just leave."

"Mia, don't say that about yourself," Eli's voice cut in.

"Don't tell me how to feel!" Mia snapped, glaring at Eli, resentment boiling through her. She couldn't believe Eli was trying to tell her what to feel. He had no right!

"Mia, we are here for you," Eli said, taking a step forward as if to attempt to comfort her. *How dare he?*

"Why would you even try to find me?" Mia asked, the indignance of all this rushing through her in a way she could not describe. She could not let Eli bring her comfort! He was nothing but trouble!

"Mia," Eli said, pushing past Harper, trying to get closer. *Oh! He wouldn't!*

"Get back," Mia said, her voice shaking, warning him off. Eli didn't move.

"Mia, what's wrong? This isn't you." He had the audacity to point that fact out.

"Everything! Okay? Do I need to tell you again?" Mia raised her voice. Eli took a step back at her ferocity at last. "Everything is wrong. How do you think I should be feeling right now, buddy? I've only been kidnapped, taken from the place that was supposed to be safe—*safe,* Eli!—and now look where I am. You think that there wouldn't be anything wrong with how I am feeling right now? Get something right for a change, why don't ya? Do something different from what you've always done, which is make fun and play with my feelings!"

"Mia," Harper said, shocked at Mia's words.

"I don't care, Harper. He's always making my life difficult, and I don't know why he even decided to come after me. He doesn't care for me!"

68

"I don't care for you? I don't care for you?! How can you even say that, Mia?" Eli asked, crossing his arms.

Mia laughed shrilly. "All the times you pranked me, writing on my nunchucks, pretending it was a joke when Gideon told us that our parents were dead—*dead, Eli!* And you laughed! What did you do then? You *laughed!*"

"Mia, calm down," Harper said, attempting to plug her friend's emotions. Mia turned to face her.

"No, I won't *calm down!*" she spat. "I have no business calming down after all that's happened to me, and how he treated me, only to act *so shocked* when I don't want anything to do with him?"

"Mia, we've been over this. He's lost his memory! What do you expect from him when he can't remember the awful things he has done to you?" Harper tried to calm Mia.

"Yeah. I don't know anymore. I don't know if he's just playing with me or not, but he's pretty hard to forgive after all he's done."

"This isn't about me, though, Mia. This is about you," Eli butted into the argument.

"About me?"

"Yes!" Eli's voice became an octave higher than it usually was. "Yes! This is all about *you,* Mia, you! We are here to help you!"

"So, when did you ever want to help me? Huh? When have you ever had an interest in me?"

"From as long as I can remember." He said it so simply that Mia snorted. For as long as he could remember? As long as he could remember would equal a few months at most. How dare he say that to her?

"Wow, what an accomplishment! That is going to take you so far in my book!" Mia's voice dripped with sarcasm.

"Mia." Eli looked hurt, as his stupid eyes had so many times since his memory loss. "Mia, we are truly here for you."

"I can believe that Harper is here for me, but not you."

"Mia, just stop it. Stop it, okay? What do you do when someone comes to rescue you? You fight with them? Really?" Harper stepped in.

"Well, when one of them is a brat—"

"No. You are acting like a child, Mia."

"How dare you!" Mia turned on Harper, fury causing her to shake. "You're standing up for *him?* I never understood how you were both friends with Eli *and* Bryce! "

"What has Bryce got anything to do with this?" Harper asked, her eyes moistening as Bryce's name entered the conversation.

"For one, you somehow could put up with both of them!"

"Mia, I'm beginning to wonder why we came for you, if this is how you—" Harper began, but Mia interrupted.

"I'm beginning to wonder why you came too. I never understood why or how you could come back for me," Mia said, stepping back from her friends.

"Mia, I've never seen you like this. Something is wrong, and we need the old Mia back."

"Old Mia was my imagination. I made her up. I made you both up too."

"No, Mia, you didn't," Eli said, stepping forwards.

"Yes. I did. You wanna know what happened in here? *You really want to know what happened in here?* I saw a fake version of you!" She pointed an accusing finger at Eli, as if he was the reason she was here, as if it was his fault that she had been tricked with an illusion. "I saw you as a hologram, and you told me that this was a good place to be. You told me I should stay here forever and that I made up the outside world. So why should I listen to you now?"

"Mia, what?"

"Stop saying my name, Eli, alright? Just stop!"

"Okay, okay, I'll stop. You want me to just back off, don't you?"

"Yes. How many times have I told you, and you don't know how to read my signals?" Mia asked, staring at him with hatred in her eyes.

"Okay, okay," he said, stepping back.

"I'll not—"

The lights in the room flickered. They all looked up. Silence filled the room.

One beat of silence, two beats, then a *click!* All the lights in the maze turned off.

Chapter 9

Darkness swallowed Mia as if a big whale had just engulfed her, dragging her down to the deep depths of the infinite ocean. Her ears pounded in the sudden silence.

"Mia?" Harper's voice called. "Mia, you're still here, right?" Her voice was quiet, afraid to speak up, to speak too loudly.

"Yes," Mia whispered, speaking up despite the dreadful fight she had just had with her friends, some of her only friends.

"Has this…" Eli cleared his throat. "Has this happened before?"

"Being stuck in a maze with you? No. No, it has not."

"Mia, I mean…" Eli faltered. "I mean have all the lights turned off on you before?"

"No," Mia said, resigned to answering his question. She couldn't make herself any less angry at this boy. The way he had treated her showed he did not deserve grace. "Mia, where are you?" Harper asked.

"Right here. Like I would walk away in the dark." As if she had not done just that several times, walking through dark rooms, from dark to light, dark to light, again and again, all by herself. She had shown over and over again that she did not need any help. No help at all. She could do this alone.

"Right, uh, should we, um, group together as to—to not get separated?" *Eli? Really? How awkward can you make it?*

"Wow, Eli, what a suggestion," Mia said, letting the sarcasm slip out.

"Mia, he actually has a pretty good point. Eli—Ah! Oh, it's just you. Mia, follow my voice."

Mia rolled her eyes so hard that it hurt. *Ugh, protective friends.* Mia inched forwards.

"Over here."

"I can't feel you yet." Thank goodness Harper said that and *not* Eli. Mia continued creeping into the unknown darkness until she bumped into someone.

"Hey." Eli's voice sounded in front of her. *Of course I would bump into Eli.* Mia stopped herself from blindly attempting to slap him in his face.

"Found you!" Mia reluctantly attempted to be playful, trying not to hold a grudge against him, at least for the time being.

"So, uh, should we see if moving to a different room will bring the lights on?" Mia asked.

"Sure, why not?" Eli asked.

Mia moved her hands about until she gripped Harper's shoulder.

"Why don't you lead the, um, way, Mia?" Eli asked.

"Because she knows this place better than we do?" Harper asked. "Sorry, that was a little evil of me to say," Harper quickly amended what she had said.

Mia gave an exaggerated sigh. "Okay, folks, shall we move instead of being in this weird three-way relationship type thing?"

She felt Eli shift awkwardly. Mia smirked, satisfied she had made Eli feel something other than cocky.

"Um, sure," he said, shuffling his feet forwards.

Mia moved forwards half an inch. Harper's hands found Mia's wrist and squeezed, almost painfully tight.

"So, let's take it one step at a time," Mia said, sounding silly even to herself.

"Weird thing for you to say—sorry," Eli said, apologizing instantly, as if he had something called 'sympathy.'

"Okay, let's move."

The group moved oh, so slowly. One little step, waiting an agonizingly long time for Eli and Harper to catch up with their slow pace, then another step, then another.

"That's right," Mia said, her voice high-pitched. "One little baby step at a time."

"Mia, really?" Harper said. "We're in this mess with you, you know."

"Wow, Harper, it's like I *asked* you to come." Mia couldn't keep it within her anymore.

"Ouch," Harper said. Then, clearly trying to brush it off like it didn't bother her, she added, "Slow and steady is a good idea."

"Okay, you two," Eli said.

Mia was appalled. "You're trying to break up what Harper and I are talking about when you were always the one who—"

"Mia!" Harper butted in. "Let's just move."

"Okay, slow and steady wins the race I guess, right?" Mia asked, jabbing one last attempt at an insult to Eli. He had always been a slow runner, even for the average person's standards. He could barely run without gasping for air like a fish out of water.

"As long as we don't run, we'll be fine," Harper said, her hand twitching on Mia's wrist.

"Wow, are you two bullying me on my running skills?" Eli asked, a fake whine in his voice. The trio crept around the room until Mia bumped into a wall.

"Well, we got somewhere," Eli had the audacity to comment.

Mia grunted, unable to disagree. They had made it *somewhere*, if not where they wanted to go.

"Feel around the wall for a door frame; each room has a door on each wall, so we should find the door eventually." The group tip-toed across the wall, fingers crawling like spider's legs, carefully looking for a turn in the wall to indicate a doorway in the middle of it. There had to be one. There had been one in all the other walls this maze place had. There would be an end, and maybe this was it. But then Mia's hands brushed a corner.

"Here," she breathed, awed that she had stumbled upon a doorframe in the dark.

"You found a doorframe?" Eli asked.

Mia snorted. "No, I found a flower growing in the dark room. Of course I found a doorway!"

"Mia, can't you give it a rest?" Harper asked, clearly exasperated.

"No," Mia said, whiny even to her own ears.

"I guess I earned it," Eli admitted.

Mia would have stared at him, but she couldn't see him in the dark.

"Excuse me, what?" Mia asked.

"Yeah, I mean, I don't remember any of it, but it must have been ba—"

"This darkness is getting too much, let's just…" Mia moved through the door frame, and the ground was no longer under her feet.

Chapter 10

Mia's voice was non-existent. Harper's shrill voice filled the air with a shriek.

"Woah," Eli gasped. Obviously, she had pulled the two down with her.

The thing about falling is it usually stops suddenly. It's either a short drop, or a large drop where you break your legs upon landing—if you land at all. Mia wasn't sure which one she preferred, not that she had a choice.

Falling through darkness was something quite different. She had never experienced anything like this, where her feet felt no solid ground and the wind whipped in her hair, making it stick straight up. Harper's fingers became painfully tight upon her wrist.

"Harper, my wrist," she said, trying to twist out of Harper's painful grasp. Her hand tightened its grip. "Eli, I can't believe I'm saying this, but can you let Harper dislocate your wrist rather than mine?"

"Um, we are falling through the air and you are asking me to—"

"Eli!" Mia's voice rose in pitch.
"Okay, okay. Harper, here, my wrist, squeeze it to death."

Harper's laugh was weak, but her grip loosened on Mia's wrist and gave her a bit of relief, though it was hard to really feel relief when she was still falling, falling, falling who knows where. The fall seemed like it would never end, but of course, most things do come to an end, and all at once, the group was on the ground. No pain, no screams.

"What?" Eli's voice sounded

The light came, slowly at first, then all at once. Mia's eyes adjusted to see an enormous, white room, unlike the black walls that had surrounded her for the past few hours.

"Now what?" Eli asked.

"I don't know." Harper finally let go of Mia's wrist, but she still clutched Eli's. He awkwardly patted her hand, still so tight on his wrist. Her fingers loosened in the slightest. Eli gently pulled his wrist free.

"Okay, okay," Eli said, looking around. "We got this. We, um…"

"We need a plan of sorts," Mia said, stepping forwards.

"A plan? How are we supposed to have a plan?"

"A plan is better than no plan," Mia pointed out. "So, what now?"

"We ought to take in our surroundings first," Eli said, looking around the large, white room that stretched on and on. The whiteness seemed to continue forever. The walls stretched on and on. The walls rose high, as if they were surrounded by that horrible Brick Wall again with no ceiling in sight. Yet Mia could tell that they were still indoors.

Mia raised her eyebrows at him. "Wow. Fantastic, Eli. Let's take a quick look around. Oh, would you look at that! We are in a white room, instead of black rooms with doorways."

"Mia, can you—"

"No." Mia rolled her eyes.

"We are getting nowhere," Harper said, breaking the argument.

"This is true, Harper. We are standing in the middle of a white room that seems to be long and has no exit that we can see. I wonder where we would be going if we walked anywhere?"

"I've just about had it with your sarcasm, Mia," Harper said, planting her hands on her hips. "You realize the situation we are in right?"

"The situation that *we* are in?" Mia asked, enunciating the 'we.' They would not be there with her if they did not try to rescue her, and now there were three that needed to be rescued.

"Harper," Mia said, ignoring Eli. "How did you find me?"

Harper looked at Mia. "Oh, well, Eli kinda, uh…"

Eli's face turned red. "Yeah, it was, um, my fault." "What happened? What did Eli do now?" Mia asked, smirking slightly despite the situation the group was in.

"I kinda followed some guys who said your name because—"

"Harper. Harper, honey."

Harper's head snapped up, her eyes dilating in a way that Mia had never seen.

"Harper?"

"Mother," Harper whispered to the voice that had reverberated around the room saying her name softly, as only a mother would. "But, but—"

"Harper, come over here. I've got something for you," Harper's mother's disembodied voice came from somewhere. It had to be a hidden speaker; there was no way the voice could permeate the room.

"Harper, I need you."

"Mother!" Harper's eyes brimmed with tears. Mia looked at her, her eyes caving in sorrow, the video of her, Harper's, and Eli's parent's dying flashing in her mind.

"Harper, please."

"Mom! I'm coming!" Harper called, running, her feet much, much slower than the way Mia's feet pounded the ground.

"Harper, wait!" Mia called. Mia caught up with Harper in a heartbeat, not panting in the slightest.

"Mom, Mama, Mother!" Tears streamed down Harper's face.

"Harper," Mia said.

"Guys," Eli's voice came.

"Harper, stop," Mia snapped.

"Mom, I'm coming," Harper gasped between tears.

"Harper, I'm over here, love," Harper's mother's voice said.

"Harper, I can tell you." Mia reached for Harper's shoulder. "I can tell you this voice is not really your mother!"

"How do you know that?" Harper turned on Mia, anger in her watery eyes. "I haven't heard my mother's voice in years! How could she be speaking if she wasn't alive?"

"I… I don't know," Mia said. "But I can tell you this: it's not real. This room lies to you, this whole place lies to you."

"Mia, you know, you're not always right!" Harper shot at Mia. Mia stepped back, appalled that Harper would speak this way to her. Harper had never snapped at her before.

"Okay, you're right, but I know this place—"

"You know this place better than I know my own mother?"

"They're dead!" Mia shouted, her voice rising in irritation. "Our parents are dead! Okay? You understand that, right? They died years ago!"

But then… how did those voices sound so exact to the person they replicated? But if there was no voice recording of them, how had Mia witnessed the deaths of her parents? How was there any way possible that she had seen her parents' deaths? They hadn't been… Had they?

Mia blinked, unable to say anything else to her distraught friend.

"Harper?" Eli's soft voice came from behind Mia. Mia turned, stepping back to give Eli some space. *What is wrong with me?* Was she actually giving Eli some space to intervene? She hated Eli, there was no way…

"Harper, I'm sorry."

"Harper, honey, please. I need your help." Harper's mother's voice filled the room.

"Mama." Harper looked up, eyes wild.

"Harper, it's not real. It's not real," Eli said, placing a hand on Harper's shaking shoulder.

"Mia." Mia froze in her spot. "Mia, honey." Her mother's voice echoed through the room next. Mia felt her eyes dilate. "Mia, come here, honey," Her feet began moving.

"Mia, no, don't," Eli tried to stop her.

"Mia!"

"Mom, I'm coming!"

"Don't you dare run," Eli said. "I'll never be able to catch you if you run." He reached out his hand.

He'll never be able to catch me if I run, went through Mia's mind. She knew what she must do.

"Mia, no," Eli pleaded, but Mia was off, running blindly, trying to find her mother.

"Mia!" Harper chased after Mia. "We'll find them together," she said.

"Yes." Mia grabbed Harper's hand, tugging her along as she ran.

"Guys!"

Eli is always tagging along after me. "Don't stop for him," Mia whispered in Harper's ear as the two ran in unison, their feet moving in sync. Harper's feet, for once in her life, kept up with Mia's.

"Where are we going?" Harper asked, the tears drying on her face.

"No idea," Mia said, a smile broadening on her face. "Away from Eli is all I know."

Harper chuckled. "He's always tagging along, isn't he?"

Mia looked at Harper, surprised that she would talk like that about Eli. Mia was the one who was supposed to say that.

82

"Wow, Harper, look at you!"

"What did I say?" Harper asked Mia, giggling as she tripped over her feet.

"You said something bad about Eli." The two looked behind them, giggling as Eli's feet pounded slower, falling behind.

"Wow." Harper chortled. "Never saw myself saying that,"

"I mean, you never say anything bad about him, and I never in my life could imagine you saying anything bad about Eli," Mia said, loud enough for Eli to hear.

"I don't like saying it."

"Mia, I'm over here," Mia's mother's voice said. Mia's feet turned and she ran to the right. Harper's breath was coming out heavier.

"Mia. Mia! I can't keep up," Harper gasped, her chest heaving in and out.

"But we are almost there, Harper!"

"I can't keep up, and I don't see her anyway," Harper said, her steps slowing so that Mia was dragging her along. "Mia, let go," she gasped.

"No, we're going to see our mothers!" Mia said. "Don't you want to see them?"

"Mia, come here please. You're not far now," her mother's voice encouraged her.

"See? We are almost there," Mia said, tugging on Harper's arm.

"Mia! Let go!" Harper tried to get out of Mia's grip. "I don't want to do this anymore."

"No, Harper, we're going to see our parents!"

"I don't see them!" Harper said.

"But they are here! I hear them. You hear your mother too! You started this; you're coming!"

"I am not!" Harper yelled, jerking her wrist out of Mia's grip, stopping where she was.

Mia whirled to face her.

Chapter 11

"**You** started it!" Mia yelled.

"You wanted to come too!" Harper pointed out.

"Our parents are not even there!" Mia yelled.

Harper blinked at her. "I was the one who said that! How stupid can you be?"

"I'm not stupid!" Mia shot back.

"Well, why did you say *that* then?" Harper asked.

"Well, I..." Mia stopped, unsure what she was going to say next.

"Harper." Eli finally caught up to them, gripping a stitch in his side. "Mia. Stop it," he said between gasps. "We need to work together to get out of here."

"No, we don't." Mia turned on Eli. "We can't possibly get out of here."

"How do you know?" Harper challenged. "We got in here to save you. To save *you,* Mia. How can you turn away from us just like that?"

"I'm not 'turning' from you guys, I'm just saying that—"

"That you don't think there is a way out. But if there is a way in, then there is a way out," Harper said.

"I've been here for I don't know how long, and there is no way out! There is no way out! We will never, ever get out, and now because you and Eli thought it was a good idea to come find me, you are both stuck here with me!"

"Well, you're repaying us so well for coming to find you, it seems like you really wanted us to come find you, right? You so wanted to get out of here that you—"

"Harper, Mia," Eli attempted to plug the fight.   "The first thing you did when we came back was get mad at us and ignore us. Why should we want to help you then, huh?" Harper asked, her hands going to her hips.

"Well, for the millionth time, I did not ask you to come to me."

"You don't want help then I guess!" Harper shrieked.

"I never asked for it!" Mia broadened her shoulders, towering over Harper. "I never asked for help; I don't need help!"
"Oh, well, then I guess Eli and I will get out by ourselves! So much for helping you! Why did we even bother to come help?" Harper snapped.

"Well, I don't know!" Mia snarled.

"Hey, both of you, calm down," Eli snapped.

"I will not! You will not tell me what to do, buddy!" Mia snapped. "I didn't ask for either of you."

"I bet you wanted help at first, but now I guess you don't," Harper said, her eyes blazing with anger.

"Go then!" Mia said, her body beginning to shake, both from the hunger pains filling her and the emotions that had been bubbling up for the past hours.

"Mia, you don't mean that," Eli said.

"Like you know that," Mia snarled. "You think you know *everything* there is to know about anything. You think you know me, but you have no idea what I've been through."

"You're right, I don't know," Eli said, his face serious for once in his life.

"What?" Mia asked, startled. Had Eli just said that she was right?

"I don't know what it was like for you, but what I do know is that there was no way you didn't want help. You are saying now that you do not want help, but I believe otherwise. You say the opposite of what you really want because you are so 'high and mighty,' you don't think you need any help other than what you can give yourself. You are selfish. How did I even fall for you before?"

"Excuse me, what? Fall for me?"

"It was quite obvious," Harper butted in. "He fell for you hard, and you hated him no matter what he said. That's no way to treat someone who is trying to mend his ways."

"Well, then you can both leave," Mia said, looking from one to the other.

"No. We will not. You are always saying the opposite of what you need. You need help, Mia," Eli told her. "We are here to help you, whether you like it or not."

"No," Mia said, crossing her arms like a little child. She didn't care. It didn't matter what he was about to say, or not say. She'd had enough of him. She was done, done, done. "I'm done with the both of you!"

"Mia, I'm not going to listen to you." "You never listen to me," Mia said. "Yes, I do.

But for now, you're being ridiculous. I
think this room is doing something to you,"
Eli said.

Mia blinked. "What room?"

"Um, this place we are in," Eli said, as if Mia should
know what he was talking about—though she clearly did not. She
was beginning to lose the thread of the conversation, as if
someone was snipping the string again, and again, and again,
until there was hardly any left.

"It's not a room, it's the world we live in," Mia said,
pointing out the obvious, for there would be no way out.

"Mia, stop being such a Debbie Downer," Harper
demanded, stomping her foot.

"You're the one making all this insufferable! I was doing
just fine alone!"

"Well, if you hate me that much!" Harper turned on her
heels.

"Harper," Eli protested.

"Eli," Harper whined.

"I've had it." Mia stormed off.

"Mia," Eli said. Mia could feel his indecision while he
tried to figure out who to go after.

She stared straight ahead. If *Harper wants to be
obnoxious, let her be obnoxious.*

"Mia, stop this nonsense," Eli panted and gasped behind
Mia. There was no way she was going to let him catch up with
her. She did not want to let that brat catch her. She continued
walking, knowing full well that he was behind her, delusional
enough to follow her.

She did not need anybody following after her when she was in such a mood. She needed to be alone, like she had been a while back. She couldn't help but need to be alone; some people needed to be alone at times. The bratty boy, Eli, never listened to what she had to say.

"Mia, we need to have a pla—"

"Plan plan plan," she slurred at him, her mind slipping. She didn't know what else to say to this boy, but she sure needed to get away from him! He annoyed her to no end.

"Mia, stop that. Snap out of it! You've been in solitude for too long when you are used to being around people, and now you can't remember how to act around peop—"

"Don't you dare insult me!"

"Oh, why do we even bother with you?" Eli's sharp tone shocked Mia, so much that she did not even bother to reply. "Why do I even bother trying to get your attention when you are always so mean to me?"

"Me? You think I'm the mean one?"

"What have you done that is nice to me? You're always yelling, snapping at me! How did I think you were hot—I mean, how did I even…" Eli trailed off, his face turning redder than his hair.

"You thought I was hot?" Mia raised an eyebrow at him.

"Y-you are one of the most beautiful girls I've ever seen," Eli said, his tone saying quite the opposite of what came out of his mouth.

"You are saying this to my face?" Mia couldn't believe his guts. Something within her stirred, the slightest, quietest stir. Maybe…

"Yes. I guess I am, and it may just be the last thing that I ever, *ever,* say to you, as you don't seem to appreciate anything that I say. I try to be nice to you, but nothing I say ever seems to connect. You don't acknowledge me as a person who really wants to be friends with you. Why is that? I should just give up on you, go find Harper, and get out of here with *her,* not you."

"Well then, that's just fine with me," Mia snarled.

"I'm out," Eli said, taking a step back.

Mia stepped back as well. "Yeah? I'm out too," she said, her eyebrows creeping   up her forehead. "I'm leaving."

"You don't care that we tried to save you, do you? Obviously not."

Mia shook her head, her heart thudding in the other direction. *Apologize, apologize, apologize!* She couldn't. She wouldn't. That's not what she did. She wasn't one to show weakness and apologize. She shook her head as she watched Eli hurrying after Harper. She shook her head again, crossed her legs, and spun around sharply to storm off even farther away from them. *That Eli, he has always - always done something stupid!* She couldn't be the only one to blame for this mess. It wasn't her fault that she had ended up here, but she would remain here forever. There was no other way for her to live this new life she had.

Mia turned around, watching Eli talking earnestly to Harper. She was alone now, the way she should be. She was meant to be alone.

They were looked up, and suddenly, something frightening reached her mind. *What if Eli manages to fly Harper back up the drop, and they leave me here alone?* As much as she wanted to be alone, she did not like the idea of being alone *here.* She shouldn't care too much—she wanted to be alone, after all— but then… But then… No, she truly didn't care. If she was alone, she could—

But you hate being alone! the little voice inside her head protested. *Not again!* Though she had just wanted to be alone, she couldn't be. But then again, things were simpler when she was… *No, no way!* There was no way that she wanted to be alone again. She took a step towards the two, who were talking one more time. She took another step toward them, worrying they would not let her back into their group after how she had treated them. Harper glanced over at her, whispering quickly to Eli, who also glanced over. Harper and Eli grasped hands. Mia jerked forwards, afraid of what the two were about to do. Eli looked up and flew into the air.

"No! Please." Mia ran to the spot where Harper and Eli had just been. "Come back!" Tears finally spilled over her face.

"Eli! You brat! Get back here! I'm… I'm s-sorry!" But he was gone. Harper was gone. The two had left her. Alone. Again. And maybe she deserved that.

Chapter 12

Mia's eyes blurred as they tried to focus on the ceiling. She didn't see Eli. She didn't see Harper. She saw no one. Her eyes wandered in front of her, finding the white room with nothing whatsoever. Eli was gone, Harper was gone. There was nothing.

She shrugged.

Well, I wanted to be left alone. And now I am alone. So why on earth was she feeling... feeling... something? There was something missing in her gut. Her feet wanted her to sit down. Mia brushed a piece of hair out of her face. She didn't know what she was going to do next. There was nothing to do in this white room that stretched nowhere.

Why was she so calm? She should not be calm at all at this moment.

She looked up again, half hoping that Eli would be flying back for her even though she knew full well that she did not deserve help. Not at all. Not one little bit. There was no way she could get out of this one; she would be stuck here forever. She could never be free ever again, stuck in this pit for the rest of her life. She did not like it here. She did not like who she had become. She fell to her knees, pain shooting through her injured leg as her body racked with sobs.

I deserve this. She no longer liked who she was. Why would she do this to herself? Why, why, why? She needed to change immediately. She had to make herself better, but it was so hard to change. There was no way that only part of you could change at a time, but she needed her whole self to change, all at once with no second thoughts. Her hands covered her face, quickly filling her palms with tears.

"I am so, so sorry," she said to no one in particular. "I know now that I am going to be alone forever, with no way to get out. There is no one who wants to help me anymore. Maybe my other hypothetical friends? Although I obviously made them up. And now I've wrecked my friendship with my best friend. I—"

"You what?"

Her head jerked up, blearily seeing Eli standing in front of her, his hair ruffled. His eyes were dark, still full of hurt from what she had said to him.

"Y-you came back?" she asked, wiping a tear from her eye.

"Yes. You don't leave your... I can't say friend, but someone you know. How could anyone abandon someone?"

"I've been so cruel to you though," she admitted, eyes cast back down at the floor and a blob of snot dripping from her nose. She wiped it, embarrassed.

"You noticed?" A sheepish look crossed Eli's face. "Well, um, I couldn't leave you. That's that, and... so... shall we go?" He held his hand out to her. *He held his hand out to her!* What was going on here? She pulled her fingers into a fist.

"If you don't want help..." He began to turn.

"No, no, fine." Mia took Eli's hand and he helped her up. It wasn't… It wasn't as horrid as she thought it would be if she ever held his hand. Not that she thought about holding his hand on a regular basis… *What is happening to me?* She dropped his hand. She didn't think he would read any signals she did not mean to give… Did she—no. She did not.

"Well?" Eli asked her.

She shifted nervously. "Where are you taking me?" That sounded stupid even to her.

"Um, up, I guess," he said. "But you'll have to hang onto me…" He blushed scarlet. Mia rolled her eyes, annoyed that he would dare say that.

"Fine." She put her hand out. Not wanting to hold his hand again, her hand gripped his shoulder.

"I guess that works," Eli said, shrugging. He looked up. Mia's body tensed as they shot up into the air.

It was a bizarre feeling, being flown upward along the same path you had fallen not long ago. She didn't like holding on to Eli for dear life, yet here she was, clutching his arm embarrassingly tight. She closed her eyes as Eli rose exhaustingly fast. She was never afraid of heights before, but now, this was all rather terrifying. Blackness surrounded them briefly, and all Mia could feel was Eli. Then… Then they were in a black room with lights on, Mia blinking hard from the sudden increase in light.

Mia promptly let go of Eli as her feet touched the hard surface. She looked around, seeing Harper. She stared at Mia, her eyes not revealing her feelings. Mia looked down, brushing her hair behind her ear. She shuffled her feet, not knowing what to say. Mia glanced back up at Harper.

"Sorry…" she mumbled.

Harper looked away. This was unusual. Harper never carried a grudge. She was always good at forgiving people.

"You make things so difficult," Harper grumbled.

"I'm sorry Harper, I-I'm stupid…"

"Hey, you're supposed to call me that," Eli said.

"Okay, fine, but just this once I'll forgive you," Harper said, pointing a finger at Mia. Her eyes revealed that she was serious. She did not want to have to forgive Mia again. Mia, being Mia, tried to make light of the situation.

"We all cooled down now? No more sissy fights?" Mia glanced at Eli, unable to be furious at him anymore, no matter how much she wanted to be fussy. He had come back for her. She didn't deserve him coming back for her, so she ought to be able to take his snarky comments from now on. Her friends had the power of leaving her in this horrible place. But now, they had to figure out what to do next.

"I'm out of plans," Mia said, shrugging her shoulders in defeat. "I really don't know what to do next, and to be honest, this case feels pretty helpless."

"We can't give up, Mia," Eli said, stepping toward her. "We can't. There must be a way out."

"But how do you know that?"

"We got in, as we've said before. So there must be a way out."

"Oh, obviously. I've been running all around this place and have yet to find a way out," Mia said, shifting her weight from foot to foot. She still felt guilty for how bratty she had been.

"I mean, we may not find a way out," she said, sorry that she had sounded so snarky.

"Should we, um, just start walking?" Harper asked, looking around the black-walled room.

"But I tried that before." Mia said.

"But you were alone then," Harper pointed out, averting her eyes. Mia knew that Harper was still sulky about their fight. Mia couldn't blame her. She had been quite awful to her friend.

"I guess we can try that," Mia said, shrugging her shoulders despite how silly it was to do what Mia had already done.

The group turned and began walking.

"We need to stick together," Harper whispered as the trio entered a black room.

Mia felt Harper's hand brush against her. Mia took her hand, as presumably Harper was also looking for Eli's hand.

"We don't want to get separated in the black room. What if one of us decided to go a different way than the rest of us?"

"You've got a point," Mia said, no longer frightened of the dark room. She had been in too many dark rooms recently to be afraid any longer.

"Thank you," Harper said.

Walking as a group was only slightly better than walking alone. In and out of dark rooms. This was not helping them get anywhere at all.

"So, what do you plan on doing next? Are we just going to keep walking?" Mia broke the long silence.

"Um, good question," Eli said.

"What if we retraced ours steps to see if there is a patt—"

"I was going to try that, but I don't think it works," Mia interrupted.

"Oh… But how do you know? You never said if you actually tried retracing your footsteps…" Harper trailed off, as if realizing she ought to not begin a new argument.

"Well, what else are we to do? There are no indications or markings on the wall to let us know if we have been in a room before, other than the lights that are snapping on and not," Eli pointed out.

"Okay, but if this walking business takes more than a day to complete, don't blame me when you guys are bored." Mia shrugged her shoulders, though the group was in a dark room and no one could see her.

After a moment of silence, Eli spoke up. "I think we began this rescue on a bad note."

"You thi—" Mia stopped her snarky remark. She was done making snarky remarks to people who were trying to help her. She needed to change herself. "Yeah, it was sorta my fault for getting upset at both of you. You are just trying to help me, and I can't thank you enough for sticking by me no matter how nasty I am to you…" She trailed off, guilt biting at her stomach.

"Yeah, we ought to not think our friends are robots. That might just help someone from being insulted." Eli grinned.

"Hey, when you've been through what I've—" Mia stopped herself once again. "Sorry, I need to stop being snarky."

"When have you been sorry for what you've said before?" Harper asked as they crossed into another light room, walking like kindergarteners in a line. She looked back at Mia.

"I'm…" Mia looked down at her feet. "I'm ashamed of how I've acted, and how stupid I've been. I plan to change," Mia said, letting her eyes go to Harper to see her friend's response. Would it be good? Would she be angry at Mia for… for what? "I'm sorry for having been so mean in the past. I never was one who took things lightly and I… I'm disappointed in myself…" She ended it quietly, her shame brimming to her face.

Harper stopped walking, putting her hand that had been holding Mia's hand onto Mia's shoulder.

"I see you are trying to change, and I appreciate that. Thank you Mia. I know it's not easy."

Eli watched the two girls, whose friendship had been dicier in the past few hours than it had ever been, mostly because of Mia. She had been the one to tilt their relationship, and she knew it. And she was sorry for it.

"This horrible thing has all been my fault," she said, looking down.

"No, it has not," Eli said, looking like he was going to put a hand on her shoulder, but then putting his hand back to his side, much to Mia's relief.

"I guess I can, um, work on how I answer people," Mia admitted, her eyes flitting away from her friends.

"Well, now that that is settled…" A woman's voice filled the room, causing everyone to jerk in surprise, looking around for the source of the voice. "Why don't we have a little fun?"

"Not you again!" Mia snarled, recognizing the voice. It was the voice of *that woman* who had brought her here.

"Oh, yes. It's me again. Aren't you happy to hear a friendly voice again?"

Mia pursed her lips. *Friendly voice? How on earth am I supposed to see this voice as friendly?* This was obviously the voice of her captor, and she must be dealt with.

"Tell me your name already," Mia demanded, crossing her arms. She assumed the woman could somehow see what they were doing, since she could obviously hear them talking.

"Well, if you insist, my name is Tris."

"So much for being mysterious," Mia snarled at her.

"And now I have a game to introduce you three to. It just might be familiar," she said, satisfaction emanating from her voice.

Mia's heart dropped in her chest.

"What—what do you mean?" she asked, taking a step back. Though she didn't know where the woman was, obviously she was able to see her and hear her, as if they were being recorded. *What a ridiculous idea!* Mia thought. *There was no way they were being recorded! But what was that she said about a game... another game? She had just escaped the game she had thought she was free from...*

"I've got a game for you," the woman repeated.

"And what if we don't want to play this game?" Harper snarled up at the ceiling.

"You've got no choice. Just like last time, I might add," Tris said.

Harper, Eli, and Mia all stared at each other, fear playing ping-pong between the three.

Chapter 13

"**Eli**! Where are you?" Eli's eyes moved from Mia's as they recognized the voice.

"Travis?" Eli asked, looking up.

"Tris!" Mia ignored Travis's fake voice. "Tris! What is this?" A flicker of annoyance sped through her as she realized what she had said rhymed. "Tris! Tell me now!" "There is no way out," Tris said.

"Eli!" Travis's voice was growing closer.

"Help! H-help me!" a new voice rang out.

"Roof!"

"Who's that?" Mia asked Eli.

Eli looked like he recognized that voice.

"Where am I?" the new voice rang out again.

"M-Maria?" Eli stuttered.

"Who's *she?*" Mia asked, indignant that he knew someone she did not.

"Help! It's all dark!"

"Roof!"

"That sounds like Emmitt!" Harper said, taking a few steps toward the dog's bark.

"Harper, wait, don't get separated." Mia said, stepping forward. "This place plays tricks on you, and we are not falling for this again."

"No, Mia, it's Travis!"

"And a strange girl! We don't know her." "Yes, we do," Eli contradicted.

"No, we—"

"Mia, she, Maria, is the girl who owns Emmitt, the dog who-who saved us the first time!" Eli ended in a shout. "Maybe he is going to help us get out again!"

"Don't be stupid," Mia said. "It's all robotic. This place does things to you."

"But if that's true," Harper butted in. "If that's true then we are all going delusional at the exact same time!"

"That's not what I…" Mia stopped. She couldn't convince her friends otherwise.

"Eli! Mia, Harper!" Travis called.

"Help me!" Maria's voice came, sounding like she was crying.

"The voices are not in the same spot, they are separated," Mia said, glancing left and right as Travis's voice came from the right, and Maria's voice came from the left.

"How are we to—"

Mia interrupted Harper. "This woman, Tris, is obviously trying to separate us by luring us deeper into the maze with our friend's voices," Mia said.

"I don't think so. I would know Travis. He is here, I'd know if he was a—not a human." Eli looked sheepish.

"No, Eli. No. You wouldn't. Why would I have been so cautious of you before if I had not been tricked a few times already myself?"

"Well…" Eli trailed off, staring in the direction of Travis's voice.

"You know how, when you first came to save me, I thought you were fake? This room does things to mimic what you think you know," Mia explained, her body tensing. How many more times would she have to say the same things? "What must I do to explain myself?"

"Okay, it's just… It's just hard to ignore your friend calling you, especially when they're calling for help," Eli said.

"I know! It's also hard to ignore your dead parents' voices who are calling your name. Even if you can't see them."

Eli looked down. "I guess you are right," he mumbled.

"But also… what if they are real? What if they really are here and we are ignoring their cries for help? We can't do that to them," Harper said, giving a logical point to this discussion. "I can't stand that idea. I can't ignore Travis; he is my friend too."

"I know." Mia looked down. She didn't want to make her friends unhappy or make them feel like they were being mean… but what else could they do? There was nothing for them but to keep on as they had been. There was no way they could—

"Roof! Roof! Awroo!" A big ball of fur barreled into the room, knocking Harper over.

"Ah!" Harper shrieked. "Help!" The dog was on top of her, and before Mia and Eli could figure out who this dog was, they saw his tongue was washing the salt-dried tears from

Harper's face. Emmitt. Emmitt had found them. They were being corralled. One. By. One.

Chapter 14

"**Well**, now we can't just stand here!" Harper protested. "We've got to find our friends!"

"We don't know this Maria person!" Mia protested, angry Harper wanted to drag her into this mess. She didn't want to help a stranger.

"But-but she's in distress!" Harper protested. "Eli and I ran into her when we were looking for you, and—"

"And she said she wanted to try and help find you," Eli said, staring hard at Mia. "So it looks like she came pretty close to finding you. Therefore, we must do something to help her! We owe her, Mia."

Mia rolled her eyes. "I don't owe her anything, not when this woman is a robotic voice. We don't know that this person really has our best interest in mind. How am I supposed to know that she wants to help?"

"Mia, I thought you said that you were changing!" Eli exploded. "You are changing, therefore you don't go on ignoring people who try to rescue you."

"I don't owe anybody any—" Mia stopped herself. She couldn't do this anymore. There was nothing left for her. She had to give in to her friend's good interests. Why would she treat her friends poorly again? She didn't like the way that made her to feel. She shouldn't continue to do it. She had to make a change, somehow, anyway.

"Okay, okay, we can go look for this 'damsel in distress,'" Mia said, rolling her eyes.

Emmitt jumped up on Eli, licking his face until he chortled.

"Stop that, buddy," he said, pushing the dog down off him. Emmitt trotted over to Mia but appeared to sense she would not like a dog jumping up on her. He was right. "Okay, where is this… this Maria girl?" she asked Emmitt. The dog jumped into the air, yelping. Mia stared at him, then the dog bolted to the right.

"Emmitt! Wait!" Eli called, running after the dog to the dark room.

The others hurried after them. Mia never would have imagined chasing after Eli.

"Oomph," Mia grunted, having run into someone.

"Who are you?" a girl's frightened voice asked.

Something fluffy bumped into Mia, a tail pounding her leg. Emmitt was obviously near them. A wet tongue touched her hand, and she jerked it back before realizing, of course, it was only Emmitt. There was nothing else in this maze that it could be.

"Are you Maria?" Mia asked the air, unable to see the person she was talking to. She knew it must be her. None of her friends were wimpy like this girl when someone bumped into them in the dark.

"Who—who are you?" the girl's frightened voice asked.

"I'll tell you when you tell me."

"Mia," Eli's chiding voice came.

Mia wanted to pout. He had just given her name away. Now how was she supposed to scare this girl?

"I-I'm Maria," Maria stuttered.

Great. This girl Eli had talked about was real. She was real and there was nothing Mia could do about her now. She didn't know quite what to do.

"I'm Mia," she introduced herself resignedly. "I'd help you up, but uh, I can't see you."

"How nice of you, Mia," Eli said.

"So we found you?" Maria asked.

Mia rolled her eyes. This girl couldn't say that she found Mia; it was Mia who had found *Maria.* Goodness, this girl was a wimp. No, no, she couldn't slip back into her old self. She was working on killing that old self.

"Um, Maria, hate to break it to you but we kinda found you," Eli's voice said. Mia snorted. He was being smart for a change. Again. *Who is this boy?*

"I guess you're right. So, you're Mia," Maria said.

"Um, you can't see me, can you?" Mia said, staring in the direction that the voice was coming from.

"No," Maria giggled.

"Let's go back to that light room we just left, shall we? And figure out what to do from there?" Mia said.

"Okay, fine, that sounds like a good idea, Mia," Eli said in a fake whiny voice that fooled no one, but maybe Maria.

"Sure, sure. Let's. I, uh, don't like the dark…" The embarrassment in Maria's voice was evident. *She must know we heard her cry like a baby,* Mia thought. Maria didn't seem like a very good person to be friends with, at least not right off the bat.

The group groped their way through the darkness toward the door from which light shone.

When they made it to the lit room, Mia turned to face this new girl. She had short, black hair that curled at the ends. Her eyes were green.

"So, why did you want to help me?" Mia asked, putting her hands on her hips.

The girl looked intimidated, taking a step back and glancing at the floor. "Um, your friends said that you needed help… so… why shouldn't I want to try and help?"

Mia shrugged. "Just seems weird that you would want to help a stranger. I wouldn't."

"Um…" Maria had no words.

"Mia, can't you just appreciate someone wanting to come find you?" Eli asked.

"Thank you for coming to save me even though we ended up saving you," Mia said, looking Maria right in the eye. Maria looked at her, then to Eli.

"How did you meet her?" Maria asked Eli.

Mia huffed.

"Long story, but behind The Wall," Eli said.

"And that wall is…?" Maria trailed off, watching the other's faces pale.

"You don't recognize this…" Harper trailed off.

"That this…" Eli couldn't finish either.

"Is a repeat?" Mia asked, sinking to her knees, no matter how strong she was supposed to be. No matter if this was a real thing or not… Mia couldn't do this again. She couldn't, she couldn't. "No, no, no!" Mia mumbled, her hands over her face.

"What? I'm confused." Maria said.

Emmitt licked Mia's head.

"It can't be; they promised us freedom!" Mia said.

"Last time it took decades to…" Eli trailed off.

"Eli, don't be an idiot. It took way longer than decades to… but … no," Mia snapped.

"You are all not making any sense," Maria butted in.

Mia began rocking back and forth, panic streaking through her. Until now, she had had some string of hope, some little light of possible freedom that she could cling to.

"It can't be." Mia looked up at them, shaking her head. "This isn't like last time," Mia said, pushing herself back up to her feet. They had promised freedom. Promised, promised, promised! "We have to find the people doing this, those in control, and get them off their pedestal! Tris! Iva! Either of you, show yourselves!"

"What is happening?" Maria was backing up from the group.

"Okay, okay, don't freak out at what I'm about to say," Mia said, taking a step towards Maria, who looked like she was freaking out at that very moment.

"Um…" Maria stammered, looking to Eli for help.

"Centuries ago, our great, great, great something or others were captured by the government and put behind a large, brick wall. The people were separated into Leagues and forced to fight and kill each other until one of us succeeded in getting the golden brick, which would set us free. We finally came up with a plan that set *two* Leagues free rather than just one. And now here we are, and we might just be repeating what happened before," Mia said in one breath, her chest heaving as she stared at Maria.

Maria was pale. "Um, what?"

"If you can't understand that, what can you—" "Mia!" Harper interrupted.

Mia stopped. "Sorry, I'm sorry. It's a lot to take in, I know, but it's just something you're going to have to accept. And it just might be happening to you right now, too."

"But-but... Eli, what is she saying?"

"Mia!" A figure barreled into her, giving her a hug from the back. Mia nearly fell over. She turned around to see Travis grinning broadly at her, Silvia not far behind him.

"Mia!" Silvia said, giving her a hug. "We found you."

"No!" Mia said, putting her hands over her ears. Travis and Silvia's faces fell.

"What? Are we playing hide and seek or something?" Travis asked, looking around. "Found you, Harper." He pointed to Harper.

Silvia swatted at his arm playfully. "Stop that."

"No. No, this isn't good. Did you hear what Tris said?" Mia asked, storming towards Travis, who backed away, his face becoming one of intimidation. "You missed the announcement, didn't you? Didn't you!"

"Mia, hey, can we—"

"Nah! We can't!" Mia slurred. "We can't do anything about this!" Her rage, fueled by the need for revenge pent up inside her, was coming out in a way that she had never seen before. "Tris!" she yelled so hard her voice hurt. "You come down here and face us!"

"You ask, you shall receive." Tris's voice filled the room.

Chapter 15

"**You** have all—well, almost all—been in this situation before." A screen flickered to life in front of the group. Tris sat there in her office. Mia's stomach churned. "We can't let people be free forever, especially when they were raised in a way that makes them vicious. Take your friend, Brynlee, for example." The screen flashed to Brynlee, who was hurrying along a street, her brother Joseph struggling to keep up behind her. "So, naturally, we must hunt you all down. One by one, or in some cases, two by two." She gave a wicked grin.

"Why is Maria here, though? She wasn't there with us last time," Mia asked, her fists clenching.

"Ah, this, yes. Yes. This I must address," the woman said, an ugly smile plastered on her face. Everyone in the room, but for Emmitt, looked at Maria. Mia took a step back, not trusting this girl who had appeared here with her friends.

"What about her?" Mia asked, narrowing her eyes at the screen, assuming this woman was able to see them.

"She is not on your side, but she is now,"

All eyes shot to Maria, who paled, white as chalk.

"What do you mean? She-she helped us!" Eli replied, standing up for Maria.

"She has been in a contract with us," Tris said." Assuming you know what a contract is."

Mia staggered backwards, putting up her fists, her muscles taut. Tears brimmed in Maria's eyes.

"N-no, this isn't true, I... I..."

"Oh, but it is. Remember the woman you signed that document with?"

"No, that was for an undercover—but—why am I here?"

"Did you read the whole contract, my dear?" Tris asked.

"N-no, of course not but I... My parents... I..."

Eli put a hand on Maria's shoulder to steady her. *Get off her, you!* Mia thought savagely.

"Exactly. You didn't read the whole contract, and now you are living up to the contract. So thank you, my dear."

"Why do you call your captives dear?" Mia stepped forward, anger rushing through her.

The woman gave a tinkling laugh. "My dear, why ask about the way I talk to people? It's my business. Anyway, this isn't a very official rule set off, so should we just start the game, since you are all interrupting so much?"

"What game?" Harper finally spoke up, stepping forward. She crossed her arms over her chest, shuddering like a leaf in the wind-breeze.

"The game I've been telling you about. This *new* and *improved* game!" The woman practically sparkled, if that was possible. "You know, the last operator of The Brick was fired, because he kind of let you all win. And we can't have that. We can't have a bunch of warriors running around New Jersey, now, can we? Take that little incident with your friend, Brynlee. That

112

told us we had to step up and make a change, and I think our vie—I think this will be a wonderful addition to your lives!"

Mia's mind whirled. She clutched Harper's shoulder for support. Her breathing became ragged, though it could be just her overthinking it.

"So now, we will begin!"

"Begin? Now hold on one moment, you—" Mia strode toward the screen, fists ready to pound the woman. Before she reached it, the screen flicked off, and Brynlee's angry cry filled the air.

Chapter 16

"**Brynlee?**" Mia was alert, spinning in a circle, trying to locate the voice of her friend. "Not Brynlee too!" She took off running.

"Mia!"

"No, Mia, stay!"

Voices shouted at her all at once, bouncing off her ears unheeded. She was unable to bear the fact that they were—what? All in some sort of *game* again? Again! After all they had been through, what they had been promised? What had been the point of capturing her first?

"Get off my brother!" Brynlee's voice came. Mia turned into a dark room, following her voice.

"Brynlee! Get out of here!" Mia screamed. She could not let Brynlee into this mess that *she* had gotten herself into. She would never stop blaming herself!

"Mia? Joseph, it's Mia!"

She had never heard Brynlee so relieved.

"Brynlee, leave now! It's not safe!" She ran into the lit room where she saw Brynlee, her hair rumpled, and her brother Joseph, who was on the floor with a nasty gash on his head.

"Joseph, are you okay?"

Joseph looked up at her blearily before Brynlee ran towards Mia, a hard look in her eyes. Mia had never been hugged by Brynlee before. Brynlee was too tough for that, but the hug showed Mia just how much she meant to Brynlee. Then Brynlee took a quick step back, staring hard at Mia, annoyance now in her eyes.

"Why are you telling us to leave? We fell through a trap door! We can't leave!"

"Brynlee, why are you here?"

"What? To find you!" Brynlee rolled her eyes.

"No, no, but you just missed—my gosh!" Mia put her hand to her head.

"Missed what?" Brynlee asked.

"The announcement!"

"What? This isn't the fair or anything. We are gonna get out of here. Hang on. Gosh, Joseph, I'm sorry." Brynlee helped Joseph get to his feet. He rubbed his head, eyes squinting. "Sorry, that stings, doesn't it?"

Joseph shrugged, as mild as ever. "I can manage. Hey, Mia," he said, giving her a small smile. "We found you."

"But you don't understand!"

"There you are, Mia! Don't you run away like that again!" Eli was entering the room, followed by the others. Maria was in the back of the group, looking like she didn't know what she was doing there.

Mia whirled around. "Don't you understand what is going on? It's Behind The Wall all over again! Just this time in a maze! How are the rest of you so calm?"

"Mia, why are you so freaked out? Take a breather," Brynlee said, stepping up towards her. "You are driving me crazy and I just got here. That's a pretty... Actually, never mind. Just stop freaking out, okay?"

"Wow, thanks Brynlee," Mia said. Then she shouted, "We are in another life and death situation! This woman gathered us all up again, and now we have to do what they say again to get out!" Tears streamed down her face, dripping down her lips and stinging her tongue with the salt water.

"Mia, it's okay," Harper said.

Harper! Of all people to tell her it was okay?

"You think this is okay?" Mia rounded on her, furious. First she came to help her, and now she is telling her the issue the whole group was in was 'okay'?

"In what way is all this okay, and how are the rest of you taking this so calmly?"

"What is 'all this,' other than we are all now in this weird place?" Brynlee butted in. "And by the way, none of them are taking whatever just happened so calmly. So tell me. What is it?"

"Didn't I tell you already?" Mia raised her voice.

"Maybe you're not the best person to explain this new, ah, situation we are in, Mia," Eli said.

Mia whipped to face him. "You dare?"

"Dare what? I'm just trying to help defuse this situation."

"This situation!"

"Mia, stop," Harper chimed in. Emmitt bounded into the room, wagging his tail with his excitement of having found them again.

"Mia, it's going to be okay," Silvia spoke up, stepping forwards with a soft expression on her face. A silent tear dripped down her face. "I know things seem hopeless,"

"Someone, just explain," Brynlee said. "I just need to know what's—"

"I need to be alone," Mia said suddenly, turning and walking out of the room. Emmitt bounded after her.

"Mia! We can't separate! It's dangerous!" Harper called.

"Let her go," Eli's voice said.

"But Eli…"

"I won't be far," Mia said, not looking back. She walked through several rooms before just standing in a black one. They were in another 'game.' They were in this situation again. She had thought they were free, but they were far from it.

Chapter 17

Mia let her eyes gaze into the black abyss of the room. She allowed her mind to spin, like one of those silly teapot ride things. Her thoughts moved so quickly that they flew off the ride and into the air, landing somewhere unknown. But it was somewhere.

She took in a deep breath as she mulled over the situation. Emmitt must have wandered off into the maze somewhere, as he wasn't trotting around, licking her hands, or jumping up onto her. She was alone in this maze-place. In another life and death situation. It would be okay.

No, it won't be okay. How can any of this be okay? Mia shook her head, laughing in exasperation. This was not some game that would just blow over. This was evil. A trouble-filled thing that Tris—and no doubt that, that *woman*, Iva—were caught up in.

"Mia?" Silvia was in the room. She didn't need to look around to see the light from the room behind her.

"Mia?" She felt Silvia's hand on her shoulder. "It's going to be alright. We'll figure this out. We've explained it to Brynlee and Joseph."

"Great," Mia said, her voice strained. "So much for you coming to help me, huh?" A tear slid down her cheek, leaving a wet trail.

Silvia let out a sad sigh. "So much for coming to help you, Mia. Now, we must work together once more. Are you ready to come back and join the group?"

"Not if Maria is still there."

"She seemed to know little, Mia. She was just as startled as we were."

"She got Eli and Harper here, though; that's what it sounded like. We can't trust her."

"We'll have to trust whoever we are here with," Silvia pointed out. "As much as we may not like it..." She trailed off. "It's what's happening, and we must accept it."

"Accept it." Mia repeated, staring into the blackness. "Accept our fate of being trapped again."

"Yes. It's not fair," Silvia agreed with Mia. Mia looked down.

"I guess we'd better face our time then." Mia squared her shoulders. Silvia removed her hand, knowing Mia had all she needed. All she could hold up inside of her was once more back. Her determination. Her spunk, her anger, her destiny.

"We're going to go smash this game in its maker's face." She turned, grabbing for Silvia's wrist and pulling her from the room, into the light.

"Great. We're a team again, but we have no competitors," Eli said, putting his hands on his hips as the group automatically circled up. Joseph rubbed his head.

"No competitors?" Mia asked, shooting Maria a look. Emmitt pranced about the circle, greeting each person in turn, then starting over again.

"Mia," Eli sighed.

"What? I'm not wrong, am I?"

"Drop it," Eli said. "We need to figure out what's next." "What's next?" a new voice came from a dark doorway. Everybody spun to look, and a boy about the same age as Eli sauntered into the room, running his fingers through his hair. He gave the group a jaunty smile. "I think I can help you with that, my friends."

Chapter 18

Great. *Another stranger calling strangers friends.*

"Who are you?" Eli asked, his eyebrows pushing up his forehead.

"Good question!" the boy said, giving a little theatrical spin and a bow to top it off, as if he were the star of a show no one asked to see… which he was. "I am Blade."

"And what is your business here, *Blade*?" Mia snarled, not ready to trust *anybody* who came close to her and her friends.

"Ah, glad you asked, glad you asked!" Blade said, stepping forwards, his cheeks dimpling with the wideness of his smile. Mia wanted so badly to step up to him, twist his nose, and hear it crack, not to mention the whimpering sound he'd surely make. "I am here for entertainment!" He spread his arms out wide. Mia couldn't take it with this boy; he was already worse than Eli.

"Run into the wall then!" Brynlee said, stepping forward and giving her chin a jerk. "Go on, let's see it then."

Blade smirked. "Tut, tut, tut. I see we have a raw sense of humor here."

"More like the personality of raw, moldering tuna," Mia shot at him, her eyes sharp as a laser beam boring holes into his skull.

"Wow, we've got quite the temper, but never you mind, never you mind," Blade said, not dropping the stupid smile he had on his face. "I've even brought some friends with me to make this fun," he said, spreading his arms out wide.

"What do you—" Brynlee was cut off as more eighteen-year-olds came out of the dark room, all in gold suits. Mia's stomach broiled, acid rising in her throat as she recalled the matching gold suits the men of League One had worn, the men that only tried to kill others and protect the golden brick.

A girl stepped next to Blade, placing a delicate hand on his shoulder. She inspected her unusually long fingernails on her other hand. "It's good to be back, now, isn't it?" Long daggers shot out of her fingernails with a clash of metal as her eyes flashed to meet Eli's gaze. Mia stepped back, recalling the man from League One whose fingernails became blades just like this girl's did.

"Isn't this wonderful now, Blade?" the new girl asked, kissing Blade's neck.

A choking sound came from Brynlee. "And who are you, little miss queen of whatever?"

"I, my lovely little chap, am Gale." Mia wanted to scream as she tossed her black, shining hair over her shoulder, retracting her claws. "Sounds like my daddy met you once, little one," Gale said, looking over at Eli and raising her eyebrows. Eli said nothing, just stared at the newcomers with something more than his usual blank expression.

122

"So, can you leave us alone now?" Mia asked, trying to make herself look bigger than she was, flexing her bicep that wasn't nearly as big as Brynlee's. She was still salty about that.

"I think," Blade said as Gale took a step back, putting her hands on her hips, "that it's time for some fun."

Gale's eyes showed evil intent as she stared at the group, a glimmer of excitement at the prospect of hurt, of pain, of even death. "My daddy has been in a bit of a mental shock after being ripped from his home, his job, and his life. He's been spending his days in a mental hospital thanks to you. He only gets visits from our host, Tris, and myself. And as the ones responsible for his demise, well, y'all get ready to play, and play hard." Her nails ejected into daggers once more as the group of gold-emblazoned teens got into a crouching position, all of them extraordinarily fit, ready to do… something.

"Um, what's going—" Maria stopped herself midsentence.

"Something's about to go down," Silvia said, pulling her hair up.

Blade sauntered forwards. He gave a wink, a wicked grin, and opened his mouth. "Get 'em," The teenagers in gold suits rushed the defenseless warriors.

Chapter 19

"Run!" Mia bellowed, turning and running.

"Easy for you to say," Eli bellowed back, face already red as he grabbed Harper's hand, pulling her along with him.

The group barreled into a black room, losing their vision.

"To the walls," Mia gasped. She was not really one for backing down and hiding, but in this case, the new teenagers had the advantage of not being in the black maze thing for as long as she had been. She pulled Eli's shoulder, and they pressed up against the wall, hearing the thundering of feet running through the room. Lights flicked on this way and that as the warriors rushed into the rooms next to theirs. Mia could hear Emmitt's barking from somewhere else in the maze, but she couldn't pinpoint where the dog might be.

Eli panted obnoxiously, as if they had run miles instead of just feet.

"You don't run much anymore, do you?" she hissed at Eli.

"Hush," Harper scolded.

The footsteps faded, and Mia relaxed slightly.

"Nice move."

Mia jumped at Blade's voice. His voice was right next to her. She felt breath on the side of her neck and tensed. A hand crept down her arm to her hand, taking it. Mia yanked her hand back, brushing it on her pants. She pushed Eli, who stumbled into Harper.

"Mia, what?"

"Move, Blade—"

"I don't think you are going anywhere," Blade said, his steel-like grip finding Mia's hand again and jerking her back.

"Get—off—of me!" Mia snarled, tugging uselessly, attempting to get out of Blade's steel grip.

"No, my darling." Blade pulled Mia close, letting his hot breath brush against her ear. She wrinkled her nose, though Blade was unable to see it.

"Mia, what happened?" Eli's voice. "Where are you?"

"She must have gone back to the other room. I'll get her," Harper's voice.

"Oh, she won't get you just yet," Blade's voice whispered as he tugged her backward, further into the blackness.

"Harper!" Mia screamed.

Blade's hand slapped over her mouth. It's grimy texture on her lips gave the sensation that he had maybe never washed his hands. She struggled against him.

"Mia! Where'd you go?"

"Don't answer that," Blade breathed into Mia's ear. She could feel his leg pressed against hers, keeping her close as he slowly backed up, forcing her to follow his footsteps.

Mia let herself loosen, untensing her arms and going limp in his grip. He grunted, trying to keep her upright. She knew this trick. She should be able to—

"Nice try," he mumbled, squeezing her so hard she yelped.

Mia twisted, thrashing about.

"Mia? Mia, what's happening?" She felt Harper's groping hand brush her hair, but then it was gone.

They scuffled in the dark, for Mia didn't know how long, until a body rammed into Blade so hard that he released her with a grunt. Mia, unsuspecting, fell to the floor. Someone tripped over her but scrambled back up, by the sound of it.

"Mia, run!" Eli! Eli must have been the one who had rammed Blade. Mia pushed herself to her feet, her injured leg protesting violently as she did so.

She bumped into someone. "Mia!" Harper's hand grabbed her arm, steering her out of the room.

"Eli!" Mia screamed, shocked by her own words. Had she really just called for Eli? *Eli?* The boy she was the most disgusted with? The boy she could never imagine being *friends* with! "Eli's not with us," Mia managed to say in all the confusion. Harper halted, her eyes squinting in the light.

"What?"

"Eli's not with us," Mia said, more impatient than she had been a moment ago.

"Mia, okay. I'll go fetch him. You just stay right here, okay? Stay here." Harper nodded, as if that would make Mia stay put.

Mia rolled her eyes. "As if I'm a puppy dog or something," she mumbled, turning as Harper disappeared back into the room. Grunts echoed out of it; the boys were undoubtedly fighting.

Lights flicked on, momentarily blinding Mia's vision.

"Welcome home!" Mia swung to her right to see Gale, her hair mussed and arms spread wide, a smile on her face just like Blade's. "We are here for just a short stay—or, should I say, you are!" Her blade-nails clanged out into position again, her eyes sparkling like an animated character's.

Mia didn't hesitate. She ran at Gale, a blazing fury rushing through her. She didn't have any weapons, she didn't have anything to use to protect herself with, but she had her fists and an anger unlike she'd ever felt towards someone. Her wits seemed to have come back to her now that she could see, now that she knew who her enemy was.

Gale slashed her fingernails down Mia's cheek. Blood rushed to the surface, oozing down her cheek. Mia threw a blind, rage-filled punch, hitting Gale's shoulder. She didn't wince. It was like the girl was a vessel of steel, one who was clearly fit and a practiced fighter. Gale clawed Mia's arm, but Mia pulled away, spinning like a ballerina to face the girl again. She dodged underneath another attempt at her cheek, thrusting a fist up to knock into Gale's chin. Gale's teeth clattered together sickeningly as she recovered her balance.

Mia moved her leg, trying to intertwine it with Gale's ankle and bring her down to the floor, but Gale hopped and escaped it, wobbling violently with her poor footing.

Mia threw a punch, managing to land it in Gale's soft stomach area.

"Oomph!"

127

A scream from Harper reached Mia's ears. Her mind turned to Eli and Harper. What was going on? Where were they? Her worries were crushed by another swipe of Gale's claws, this time down her left arm, not hard enough to draw blood but enough to make her angry. Mia pounced. She put her hands on Gale's shoulders. Gale's hands went to her neck, but Mia shook the girl so vehemently that she couldn't get a firm grip. Mia lifted her right foot and kicked as hard as she could, sending Gale falling hard on her tailbone. Her right thumb blade snapped off, causing her to snarl in pain.

The girl sat there for a moment, her hands behind her. She stared up at Mia with venom in her eyes.

"Mia! Mia, what?" Harper was there, her clothes torn in several spots, hair a mess. Eli was there too, his eyes wild.

"Let's go," Mia said, glancing back at her friends. That was her mistake.

In the slickness of a cat, Gale tackled Mia from her knees, sending her crashing hard to the floor. Mia's chin smacked the floor, her teeth clattering together. Stars burst into her vision as nine sharp blades pierced her legs. This girl was insufferable!

A pull, a yelp, and Gale was off her. She pushed herself up to see Eli had Gale in a choke hold. Harper pulled Mia away from the two. Mia's eyes widened as Gale went pale, her mouth gaping open like a fish before her eyes rolled up in her head. She went limp. Eli let her fall to the floor.

Mia's eyes flicked up to Eli. "Did you... You didn't kill her, did you?" Not that she minded; she would be glad to get rid of Gale.

"No, just knocked her out," Eli said, staring down at her.

"Let's go."

"Where are the others?" Mia asked as they left through the left-hand doorway.

"I don't know," Eli said solemnly.

"We need to find them," Mia insisted.

"I know, but where do we start?" Harper said, looking around helplessly.

Mia halted, her eyebrows furrowing.

"Mia, what is it?" Eli asked, staring at her.

"The light in the room behind us is on, so why is this light on? We should be in a dark room."

Eli shrugged. "Maybe this is a new stage in the weird maze thingy."

Mia shook her head, eyes narrowing. "I wouldn't count on that. Something is fishy here. The light pattern is changing, so maybe the lights are not a hint for the way out. Maybe…" Something filled her gut. "Maybe it's all a distraction." Mia knew this place by now. When things changed, something bad happened. And if something bad was going to happen, Mia didn't want to know what it was. She didn't need to experience it. She'd already had enough bad things happen to last her ten lifetimes. Mia let her eyes wander. She stopped, glancing first to Eli, then to Harper.

"There are no other doorways here," she said.

"What?" Eli asked, scratching his head.

The idiot. "There are no other doorways here. Look around you!" Mia flung out her hand.

The places where doorways had been were now solid wall. Wall, wall, and wall. All at once, a great, big, *thunk!* caused the three to jump, flinging around to see that a brown, everyday door with a lock had sprung up where the empty doorway had been a moment ago.

"Um…" Harper stepped back from the door, her eyes darting this way and that. Mia approached the door, Harper whimpering nervously. Mia opened the door and stepped inside, Eli and Harper reluctantly following her. When the door swung shut, an uneasiness filled Mia.

Thunk! Thunk! Two beds appeared, fully made, with night stands and a lamp next to each. A thin wall rolled up from the floor to the ceiling, creating a nook where another fully-made bed popped up, this one with blue sheets and comforter.

The three stared, shocked.

"What. Was. That?" Eli asked.

Mia didn't know. But she did know she didn't like it. Mia backed toward the door, fumbling for the doorknob.

"Maybe the game is trying to tell us to get some rest," Harper said, staring at the bed with the purple comforter.

Mia shook her head. "Are you out of your mind, girl? We can't sleep here."

"It seems safe enough," Harper argued. "There is a door with a lock. We will be protected from those other kids," she reasoned.

"No. We've got to find our other friends, or at least…" Mia drew herself all the way up. "I have to go find our friends. You both can stay behind if you want to, but there is no way I am abandoning the people who came to help me." She gave Harper a definite look, one that challenged her to argue.

Harper glanced back at the bed, then back to Mia. "Okay, okay," she said. "I'd never abandon the others either. Let's go."

Eli put his hand on the door, hesitating.

"You sure about this?" he asked Mia.

"Very sure," Mia said, crossing her arms.

Eli opened the door, and there stood Blade.

Chapter 20

Eli stumbled back, bumping into Mia in shock.

"Good morning, friends!" Blade greeted as he moved his hands in front of himself, showing them the sword he was yielding. "The time is now 7:58am and it's time to have some fun!"

"We are not friends!" Mia yelled, fury overcoming her logical thoughts.

"Mia, run!" Harper shouted. But Mia couldn't move. She couldn't comprehend this nightmare that was upon her.

"I saw what you guys did to my girl, Gale, and I must say, you will pay for that one." Blade took an ominous step into the room. Harper had the good sense to put her body in front of the door so it would be impossible for Blade to shut it and lock them in.

"Who shall we start with." Blade looked appraisingly at each.

"Who are you exactly?" Eli asked.

Blade was startled. "What?"

"Who even are you? Where are you from?"
Blade let his gaze linger on Eli, longer than Mia felt comfortable for. "I don't need to tell you," Blade said simply,

running his finger along the sharp end of his sword. He swiped it so close to Mia that her hair moved. She blinked, just then remembering her bleeding cheek. She brushed it with her shirt sleeve, leaving a good smear of blood.

"That's my girl," Blade said wickedly, his teeth sharper than usual as he grinned maliciously. He stuck his tongue between his teeth. "She did that to you, didn't she?"

Mia refused to answer this, this monster. There was no way that this boy, this thing, was a real human! He had to go, and fast.

Blade put his sword up to her neck so it was diagonal as he stood before her.

"Mia," Eli said.

Mia's hand twitched, she let her gaze linger on Blade. "You will not take me this easily," Mia said.

Blade's eyes glowed. "Oh, but I think I will."

The blade pressed into her neck a little further. Mia knew what she had to do.

"Okay then." She closed her eyes. "Take me." Nothing happened.

Mia cracked an eye open. "Well? You gonna end me or aren't you? Are you too weak?"

"Mia," Harper hissed, as if scared Mia would really do nothing.

"By the way, it's two against one," Mia rolled her eyes.

"I've got the weapon," Blade said.

It's working!

"Yeah, that's right." Mia allowed her posture to slump, then a big *thunk* sounded as the sword clattered to the ground. "I knocked him out," Eli said, flashing a grin.

"Is that your signature move or something?" Mia asked, grinning despite herself.

"I guess so. Should we lock him in?"

Mia nearly laughed. *What was happening to Eli? Why was he nice?*

"That seems kinda cruel..." Harper trailed off.

"Harper!" Mia exclaimed indignantly. "That boy tried to kill us, and you are wondering if we *shouldn't* lock him in, is that right?"

"Well, I—"

"No! We certainly should, if we can get rid of one more scoundrel."

Blade stirred, his hand twitching.

"Okay, okay, you win, let's just get out of here," Harper said, backing away.

The three slipped from the room, locking and shutting the door behind them as they went.

"Okay, okay, what now?" Eli asked as he looked around the black room that was somewhere in the maze.

"Well," Mia said, putting her hands on her hips, "we obviously leave this place."

"I don't know about that, Mia." Harper scrunched up her face. "I don't know if it's a good thing to go out there with, with those other... with those other..." She trailed off.

"I know, but what choice do we have right now? I know it's freaky out there with those other kids, but we must keep moving. I think every time we stop is when we are cornered by them. It's dangerous," Eli said.

"But we don't even know how to get out of this place! We were given no rules!" Harper cried, tears blossoming in her light purple eyes.

"Because we have to. We can't just sit here!" Mia said. "If we sit here, the room gets to us; if we don't, we're in the open. What choice do we really have? This is not Behind The Wall, Harper. This is different, very different."

"But—but—"

"It's scary, I know," Eli interrupted Harper's plea. "But Mia is right." He looked at her, ready for something. "We must move. There is no point in sitting around waiting for them to kill us. Why should let that fate march right up?"

Harper glanced back at the door, wondering if Blade was awake now, trying to get out, or still unconscious.

"Okay." She nodded and took a deep breath. "Okay then, let's go. Let's do this." She led the way.

Chapter 21

The group crept towards the dark doorway ahead of them.

"Where do you think the others are?" Eli asked, his voice low.

"They could be anywhere at this point," Mia said.

"Thanks, Mia," Harper said, rolling her eyes.

"You are so welcome, Harper," Mia said, giving her a sarcastic, winning smile.

The group entered a dark room. The trio moved close together, holding each other's shirts in order to stay together. Mia's foot hit something hard. She nearly stumbled, grabbing on to Harper to keep herself from falling.

"What is it?" Harper asked, her body trembling. "I think I just tripped over somebody." Mia added on inspiration, just to frighten Harper, "Or on *something.*" "Mia," Eli stopped himself.

"I'm going to make sure it's not one of our people," Mia said, crouching down and feeling around on the ground with her fingers. She moved them across the floor like a cautious spider's legs until they met the body. She hardened her face in concentration. She let her fingers slide, though it felt strange to do so, over the person's face, to her hair, then back to her face.

"Silvia," she gasped. "Silvia, can you hear me? Where is Travis? Why isn't he with you?" The body stirred, letting out a low grown. "Silvia? Silvia, can you hear me?"

"What?" Harper gasped. "It's Silvia?"

"Yes. Harper, help me. We must get her to the light room so we can see her." Together, the three of them managed to lift Silvia in the dark and inch their way toward the light.

Mia stared at Silvia, saddened by what she saw. She had a black eye, and Gale's claw marks ran down the right side of her neck.

"Gale," Mia growled, her fists clenching. "I thought *you* took care of her." Mia shot at Eli.

"I thought I did too," Eli said, looking down sadly at Silvia's motionless body.

"Silv, Silv, can you hear us?" Mia asked, gently shaking her friend's body. Silvia's eyes fluttered open, blinking away grogginess.

"Mia? You're alright?" she croaked, trying to sit up, but she was clearly weak from whatever had happened to her.

"As alright as I can be," Mia said, giving her friend a small smile. "What happened?"

"Gale," Silvia mustered, attempting to sit up again, succeeding with Mia's help.

"Do you know where the others are?" she asked.

"No. We were about to go look for you guys," Mia said. "Why would Travis have left you there?"

"He didn't," Silvia said quickly, shaking her head and attempting, but failing, to get to her feet. "He didn't. He wouldn't. Something must have happened that he couldn't avoid."

"Well, he did—"

"Eli," Mia snapped, giving him a shove—not as hard as she might have at one time, but a shove nonetheless.

"Once you feel up to it, we can go find the others," Mia said, brushing some hair out of Silvia's face. The girl shuddered.

"That Gale though, she's tough."

Mia nodded. "I hate her already."

"We'll get her again if we have to. We've done it once," Eli said.

"Barely," Mia added.

"Hey, what can I say?" Eli beamed.

Silvia got up with Mia's help, her knees knocking together.

"I-I'll be okay in a moment," Silvia muttered, taking a shaky breath.

"Right," Mia turned to Eli and Harper, who still supported most of Silvia's weight. "What way do we go?"

"I say we just pick a direction and go for it," Eli said, shrugging. "What else is there to do? It seems that there is not really a good way to plan anything here anyway, and with danger around each corner, there is as much of an opportunity for more danger around one as the next."

"Wow. Thanks a bunch, Eli," Mia said.

"You are *so* welcome." Eli grinned.

"Ready, Silv?" Mia asked, looking over at Silvia, who gave a shaky smile.

"Yeah. Ready to face the hordes."

The group crept onwards. Once more, Mia went through room after room after room, but this time, at least, she had friends. This time she knew she was wanted, even if she was facing even more danger than before.

This time, there were enemies afoot.

Silvia stumbled in the next bright room the group entered. Mia paused, helping her to regain her balance.

"I'm sorry," Silvia said, a tear sliding down her brown cheek. "I'm so sorry, I'm ruining everything. You should just leave me here. If I hadn't gotten hurt—"

"Don't even say that," Mia interrupted, a flash of defiance going through her. Though the group would move easier without a girl who was half out of it, there was no way Mia would leave Silvia here. Not after she had worked so hard to get here to try to save Mia. "We are *not* leaving you here," Mia said again, stubbornly.

"But—"

"Hush, Silvia. You can take a seat and rest if needed. We can wait." Mia lowered a resentful Silvia to the floor.

"I'm fine," Silvia pouted.

"You are *not fine,*" Mia retorted.

"Mia's right," Eli said. Mia stared at him. "You need to be careful not to exert yourself."

"You sound like a medic." Harper giggled, covering her mouth. Mia raised her eyebrows at Harper's childishness.

Mia allowed her eyes to survey the room while they waited for Silvia to rest. Her eyes found another new door, her eyebrows furrowing. She didn't hesitate to go toward the door; it was just like the bedroom that had appeared out of nowhere right in front of them.

"Mia, where...?" Mia didn't stop to look at Eli. She kept walking towards the door. She had to know what was behind it. It felt like something there that would help them.

She opened the door without hesitation, and she was right!

Behind the door was a long, deep closet, not unlike the closets from Behind The Wall. Weapons of all kinds cluttered the closet: bows and arrows, swords, guns and spears. Anything a warrior could want. But the one thing that drew Mia's eyes, the one that made her gasp with tear actually welling to her eyes, was the nunchuck that hung on a gold hook. She reached for it, but hesitated.

Something's not right here. Mia took a step back, her hands shaking.

"Mia, what?" Eli was right next to her, staring in disbelief at the closet of weapons.

"I-I don't know where this came from," Mia managed. "It must have just appeared, and look." Mia pointed to her nunchuck, the one that was unmistakably hers.

"Mia..." he breathed. Other times, this would have infuriated her. how dare he say her name like that? —but now she merely twitched her wrist.

"We actually have a chance now!" Eli bounded toward the closet of weapons.

"Eli, I don't think—" But Eli was already reaching towards Mia's nunchuck, his hand closing around it. He turned, his face beaming with joy, to hand it to Mia and... nothing

happened. Mia took her nunchuck, the one she hadn't held in—
how long?

"But… but…" she stuttered. Eli pulled Harper to the
closet, waving his arms around in glee.

"We actually have a chance now, Harper! Don't you see?"

The nunchuck was old and familiar at the same time. The
faded words that Eli had so mischievously written on it in
permanent ink years ago—*My Chucky*—still marred the
blackness of the nunchuck. Mia didn't remember where in the
house she shared with Brynlee and Harper she had left it the day
she… she last left it. But she knew it had been safe. Now here she
was, holding it in her hand and staring at her lost joy. She was
reunited with it at last.

"Mia?"

Mia's eyes jerked up to see Eli. His eyes stared into hers,
as if trying to read her thoughts.

"Mia, you okay?" he asked.

Mia blinked. "Yeah, yeah, I'm fine. We should stock up
with as many weapons as we can carry." She brushed past Eli and
into the room briskly, as if she wasn't thrown off by the
appearance of her nunchuck. As if she wasn't getting emotional
for the past. As if… She put her nunchuck in its rightful place in
her back pocket. Its old familiarity threatened to bring back
memories to overwhelm her, but she shook them off. She could
not afford to be sentimental about the past now. Not now, not in
this situation that they were in.

Mia grabbed an old bow and the quiver full of arrows next
to it. She had never been an archer, but she felt that if there was

any other weapon she could get the hang of, it was archery. She didn't like the idea of swinging around a stupid sword.

Out of the corner of her eye she saw Eli pick up, with awe, the sword that he had used Behind The Wall. Geez. How did the people get their hands on those weapons? It was like they knew those who had put them in their last situation.

"Eli, don't you think this is a little suspicious?" Harper asked, not daring to touch the weapons.

"I don't like this," Silvia said, having made it to her feet and over to her friends by herself.

Eli shrugged. "Even if it's part of a trap—"

"Oh, even *if* it is part of a trap," Mia mimicked. "If, if, if!" She threw her hands up. "There is no *if* at this point—sorry." Mia squeezed her eyes shut. "The fact is that I'm trying to change. So if we are in a trap, this is just like another level of the said 'game.' Is that what you're trying to say, Eli?"

Eli's eyes studied Mia. "Yeah," he said after a moment. "Yeah, that sounds about right."

"They would do that to us," Harper grumbled, kicking at a sword. "I don't want to touch a weapon again." Her eyes flitted to a long dagger hanging on the wall. "Especially not that." Harper turned away, a sob escaping as she covered her mouth with her hands, desperately trying not to show that she was crying.

Eli put a hand on her shoulder. "It's okay,"

Harper snapped. "It's not okay! Bryce is gone! *Gone,* Eli! And he won't be coming back!" Harper gasped. "Oh, Eli, I'm sorry." More tears streamed down Harper's face, and she shoved her way out of the closet so she could cry with her back towards them.

142

"Oh, Harper." Silvia limped after Harper.

"She's still not over him, is she?" Mia asked, glancing back at Harper, not having the patience to console another sobbing girl at the moment.

"Mia, you know they were close friends. He was my friend too, you know," Mia grunted.

"You didn't like him though, did you?" Eli asked.

"I didn't like you then either, though," Mia said, avoiding eye contact as she picked up and inspected a dull dagger. Brynlee would not have approved. "But no, I didn't like him much. When he wasn't tagging along with you, he was taking Harper from me."

"Huh?" Eli scratched his head. Mia wanted to roll her eyes so hard it would hurt, but she stopped herself.

"Harper started hanging out with you and Bryce a few months before we won. She was just kinda friends with him at first, as you probably know, but then suddenly she stopped spending as much time with me and spent it with *Bryce*. But you know, it's whatever." Mia waved it off, tossing the dagger to the ground with a clatter. She glanced back at Harper, who was in conversation with Silvia.

"Silvia's good at calming people, isn't she?" Eli asked, strapping the sword to his side.

"Yeah," Mia said, watching the two converse. "That's something I was never, or may ever be, good at."

"Good trait for her to have. Travis is pretty good at it as well. I think she rubbed it off on him a little though." Eli smirked, then straightened his face. "It still stings a little that Travis went behind our backs like that. I mean, c'mon, dating a girl from a

143

different League?" Eli shook his head, picking up a gun and examining it. "I've got no idea how to use one of these." He picked up a few darts, letting them fall into a silk bag that he tied around the belt with his sheathed sword. Eli looked ridiculous, but Mia resisted the temptation to tease him. She was working on herself. She had to change.

Harper and Silvia came back. Harper's eyes were rimmed red, but she wasn't crying anymore. Eli handed her the silk bag of darts, and Harper took it without hesitation as Silvia rummaged through the weapons herself. Harper scuffed her toe on the floor, not meeting anyone's gaze. Eli lifted something else to Harper. Her eyes flickered up from the floor, widening, brimming with tears again. Bryce's dagger. Harper shook her head.

"Take it, Harper," Eli encouraged. "He-Bryce, would have wanted you to have it." Harper reached out and took it with a shaking hand, another tear sliding down her face.

"Thank you," she whispered, holding the weapon reverently.

"Wish the others knew about this place," Eli commented, looking around. "It'd be nice if we could all be able to defend ourselves."

"Well, let's hurry up and find everyone. The more brains we have"—Mia resisted glancing at Eli to sarcastically indicate that he has no brains—"the better chance we have to get out of this mess." She finished after a slight pause, where she had taken the time she needed not to be the rude woman she usually was. "Yes, let's," Eli agreed with her.

"Wow, look at you two go," Silvia said, a sparkle in her eyes.

"Silvia!" Mia blurted, appalled at her audacity.

Silvia chortled, something very unlike her quiet, ladylike personality. Mia caught Harper smirking just slightly, but Harper quickly looked back at the ground.

"Let's go," Mia said, turning to leave the weaponry.

"Let's go see what's coming for us!" Eli said, much too cheerful for the situation that they were in.

Chapter 22

The group reconvened in the room. Mia's confidence had grown after having a weapon at her side. She knew she could do anything now, no matter what this miserable place threw at her. She did not need to be a victim anymore. She would be the aggressor and champ over her enemies.

Silvia, who seemed to have, thankfully, overcome the initial pain in her injuries, walked behind her and Eli, talking with Harper in a low voice. Mia's ears picked up voices coming from the room to her left, it's light on.

"Stop," Mia hissed, holding up her hand.

"Yeah, but it'll take forever for us to find them!" Travis's voice.

"No matter. We're bound to stumble upon them eventually." Brynlee. *Brynlee!* Mia jerked into a jog, leaving the others behind.

"Mia," Eli hissed.

Mia burst into the bright room, her eyes squinting before they adjusted.

She saw Travis and Brynlee in a heated argument, not noticing Mia until she yelled "Hey!" at the top of her voice. Both friends stopped arguing and turned to face her.

"Mia," Brinlee said, relaxing instantly. "Where—"

"Siv!" Travis brushed past Mia and engulfed Silvia in a bear hug.

"What happened?" Silvia asked. "How did you not stay with me?"

"I don't even know what happened, to be honest," Travis said, pulling back from the hug and kissing her on the cheek. Mia looked away pointedly. The two disgusted her sometimes.

"I'm sorry we parted ways," Travis said, taking Silvia's hands.

"Okay lovebirds, this is not the place," Mia said, rolling her eyes at them. The two sheepishly dropped one hand, keeping the other firmly held in each other's palms.

"Sorry Mom," Travis said, giving her an un-Travis-like grin.

Mia shook her head, having none of it. She didn't want Travis giving her *any reason* to snap at him. Travis was a good guy, but when he got too affectionate around Silvia, it got, well, it got a bit too steamy in the room for Mia's comfort level.

"Okay, off to find the others," Mia said, taking a sharp turn. "We're just missing Joseph now, right?" "And Maria," Eli butted in. *Maria!*

"No," Mia turned to face Eli. "We are not missing *Maria.*"

Eli pulled his lips together before saying, "Yes, we are. She came here with us."

"Why are you sticking up for our enemy? Why? She is the one who helped get you and Harper here in the first place!

147

How in the world can you still stick up for her now, after all she's done to you?"

"But she clearly didn't kn—"

"Don't tell me she didn't know!" Mia advanced on him. "Don't you dare tell me she didn't know. She obviously knew, and by knowing, she got you and Harper here! The both of you! She is the one who signed 'the contract!' It's her fault if she didn't read whatever that is close enough. She's working for the enemy. The *enemy,* Eli! Aren't you listening to me?"

"You're not listening to me, either, Mia," Eli said stubbornly. "You saw the look on her face. She had no clue what was going down."

"She didn't read whatever that contract thingy is!" Mia's voice rose an octave higher.

"Let's just go find my brother." Brynlee walked through the group's fight, drawing the two's attention to her and away from each other. The others followed without bothering to argue. It was pointless to argue with Brynlee. She always knew what she was doing, and she refused to be swayed one way or another.

The group entered the next room, clustering close once more as the darkness engulfed them.

"Why hello, chicks," a girl's shrill voice echoed in the room.

Something sharp hit Mia's leg, causing her to stumble, then chaos erupted. Shrieks and war cries filled the room. The sound of shuffling, fighting, reached Mia's ears.

Mia had no idea what was going on, but something was. Something bad. She tussled with a masculine figure in the dark, unable to see who he was. His strength nearly overpowering her.

Mia knew she could not go on much longer in the state she was in. She hadn't eaten in, well, she didn't know how long. She just knew it would soon be too long. Her parched throat begged for water as she fought, her breath once more becoming ragged as her weakened state wailed for her to just give up the fight. But there was no way that she was going to give up on herself. She could not give up on herself.

The man, boy, whoever, gave her an enormous shove, and she fell into someone who grasped her arms, pinning them to her sides.

"I got her!" a voice said too loud in her ear.

"Let go of me!" she snarled.

The lights of the room flicked on, momentarily blinding the fighters and disorienting the pattern of the maze.

Mia made it out of her captor's grip, turning to see the burly teenager with the muscles of a bodybuilder. His scruffed black hair stood up in spikes, and when he grinned at her, his right front tooth was chipped into two pointy spears. He stuck his tongue out of the hole in his teeth and gave a little hissing noise.

"We'll get ya!" he said, his voice in between a mature, deep, male voice and a teenage gangster's pitch.

Mia threw a punch at the boy's face.

"I'm Flint, by the way," he said, grinning as he easily dogged Mia's punch. Around them, Mia's friends were fighting ferociously with the other teenagers, her friends unfortunately rusty compared to the skills they had once obtained Behind The Wall.

What's with all the weird names? Blade and Flint? Mia asked herself. But she didn't have time to linger on her questions.

A high-pitched feminine voice came from behind her. "Oh, Mia!"

Mia whirled around, her hair whacking Flint in the face as she turned. Gale.

Gale! That Girl! Mia ran towards her. Flint attempted to grab her again, but she pulled out of his grip. She needed to finish that girl. She needed to take her down. She hated that girl. Gale! *Gale!* Mia ran into her with such force that the young woman had no time to unleash her nails before she was knocked down. Gale smacked her head on the hard ground, eyes going wide. Mia didn't stop, running over the woman who had caused so much trouble. She crouched, whirling her nunchuck, awaiting Gale's next attack.

"Come and get me," she challenged, smirking.

Gale, disoriented, remained on the floor a moment too long, Eli was there in a heartbeat, drawing his sword and raising it over her. Flint ran at Mia, sidestepping Gale as he did so.

As Eli's sword came hurling down, a strange look entered his eyes. Another sword clashed with Eli's. Mia just had time to see that Blade had gotten his sword over Gale an instant before it was too late, stopping Eli from killing her on the spot. A dark look glinted in Blade's eyes.

Then Mia was too busy to see any more. A clash filled the air as Mia's nunchuck crashed against Flint's weapon of choice, a crooked dagger that was longer and uglier than Brynlee's prized possession.

"What is it that you have"—Mia gasped, her breath suddenly leaving her— "against us? What did we ever do to you?" she asked, hoping logic would win over the teenager's vicious attacks.

"You fought against our parents," Flint hissed through his crooked teeth.

"So? What's that got to do with us?" Mia gasped. "You don't have to fight us just because we were forced to—"

"League One was forced to fight too, you know," Flint said, a wicked smile creeping across his face. "You do realize you're not the only ones who have had troubled lives."

"I never said—"

"Oh, but you indicate it," Flint said, slashing near Mia's ear. "You sure indicated it." Flint swiped at her nose again.

Mia stopped fighting, startling Flint into stopping himself. The battles raged on around the two.

"You mean League One were captives just like we were?"

Flint's eyes narrowed. "What did you think they were? Monsters?" he asked, his fists clenching, trembling in his exertion.

"Um, yeah. Just kinda."

"Well, they weren't." Flint took a step forward. "They were not the least bit *monsters*.

Chapter 23

Mia stepped back, appalled that the League she had hated so much were people just like her League and Silvia's. They had been captives too? Innocent captives that had grown up fighting and killing. *Then why are their children fighting us if they were so innocent?* a little, logical voice inside her head asked.

"Then, if that's the case, why are you fighting us?" she asked, immune to the fights and shots around her

"Well, you say that we are monsters too, I reckon. If you assume League One was monsters, when in reality they were innocent adults forced into a war no one wanted to begin with, how dare you call us monsters too. Obviously, I am a victim to this crime as well," Flint said.

Mia's nunchuck went limp in her hand as his words sunk in. "You were forced into this maze as well?" she asked, her body releasing a little bit from the pressure that had been on her shoulders.

"Of course." He let his eyes linger on the ground, his shoulders slumping.

Mia took a step towards him. "You mean, you mean you were f-forced here too?" Tears, for no reason Mia could tell, stung her eyes.

Nine sharp blades wrapped around her neck. Gale.

"Hey, little missy," Gale sang. "Ready to die?"

"Gale!" Flint spoke, "I almost had—"

But Eli shoved Flint from behind, having snuck up on the two during their intense conversation.

Mia slammed her elbow into Gale's stomach, but the girl merely grunted. Mia let her knees give way, the blades scraping up her neck to her chin, which became too heavy for Gale to hold in her bladed nails. Mia fell to the floor, scooting back so she went between Gale's legs. The girl lost balance, and Mia whirled around, shoving Gale down once more. She kicked Gale's foot in sheer anger, forgetting that Gale was as much a captive as she was. Forgetting, just for the moment, that Gale was a human too.

Gale got to her hands and knees, her eyes livid with anger, and there was Blade, helping Gale up, menace in his eyes.

"You dare attack Gale again?"

Mia raised her eyebrows despite the situation, laughing as she whirled her nunchuck. "Gale is the one who attacked me first, don't forget!"

"Mia, please, listen to me," Flint's voice found Mia's ears as the battling teenagers continued to swarm them.

"Flint, not now!" Blade deterred his comrade.

"We are people too. We don't deserve this, do we?"

"Then why don't we gang up together to get out?" Mia said, a light bulb going off in her mind.

Eli took a swipe at Gale, who whirled around and became immersed in combat, slashing at him with her claws.

"It won't work that way," Flint said, dodging a swipe form Silvia, who, thinking she was helping Mia, was attempting to distract him.

"Why won't it?" Mia challenged Flint.

"It just won't. It can't," he said, jumping over Silvia's leg. Eli and Gale were still in close quarters, both fighting vigorously, sweat glistening on Eli's face.

"But, what then?" Mia asked, feeling a swipe of something nearby. She stepped closer to Flint to try and avoid the scuffle.

"We can team up. Come on, Mia. It'll be a lot easier for us to team up and escape if we work together." Flint did his tongue thing again, sticking it out so part of it poked through his tooth.

"Um…" Mia glanced over at her friends. "What about my friends?" She folded her arms.

"Oh, it'll do us all good. It will help them by having less competitors, and Silvia won't be slowing you down anymore." Flint drew closer to Mia, so close that eye contact was almost unnerving. His deep blue eyes were a darker blue than the sky. "It'll do them all good," he hissed, a little quieter than before.

"Mia, what are you doing?" Eli rammed into Flint, knocking him off balance and nearly sending him toppling onto Travis's weapon, which he was flashing at another warrior.

Mia had enough. She made her decision. Darting up to catch Flint, she looked at Eli, her eyes ablaze.

"What do you think you are doing?" she asked, anger rushing through her.

Eli took a step back, baffled at Mia's words.

154

"Mia, I—"

"Don't answer that, just don't." She helped Flint to his feet. He gave her a grateful smile.

"As I said, we are all in this together." He smirked at Eli.

"We ought to get out of here," Mia said, turning to go.

"Mia, what?" Eli stuttered.

Flint was at Mia's side, taking her hand. "Yes," he said.

A burst of adrenaline rushed through Mia.

Chapter 24

Mia left the room hand in hand with Flint. Flint was strong, his attitude right, and his hair—well, his hair was just perfect. Funny, she had never thought this way about any man before. *Especially not Eli.* She looked at him as they entered the quieter room, the giddy smile on his face not wavering. The two walked through two more rooms, ignoring the faint cry of her name.

"Mia!" rang out as Eli was detained by some of the other miraculous fighters. Mia and Flint stopped in the third bright room and faced each other.

"It's a deal, then?" Flint asked, running his hand through his already spiky black hair.

"Yes," she said, her hand cooling in the air without another hand clasped around it. This was a new feeling for her. "You had me for a second, but you made me realize we are all just people. Why should you be our enemies?"

"You are so right," Flint said, nodding. Mia noticed a small silver-and-gold sword necklace dangling from a rope around Fint's neck. It seemed familiar, but Mia took no more notice of it. "We're going to do great, and we're going to get you out of here," Flint smiled.

"What about…" Mia glanced back in the direction from which they had come.

"What about what?" Flint asked, his smile wavering for just a split second.

"What about the others?"

"What about them?" Flint asked. "They are safer without us. Less competition."

"You sure about that?" Mia asked, glancing back into Flint's amazing eyes.

He grinned, his tongue no longer sticking between his teeth. "Of course! They will have a much easier time without you! Now, let me show you the way!"

"I thought you didn't know the way," Mia commented, turning and following Flint as he began walking again.

"Oh, but that was just a ruse to make the others think I was bad," he said. "I am really just a good person."

Mia gave a small smile, her eyes flitting back to his bulging muscles. He caught her looking and flexed his right arm slightly; she glanced away, bashful of what she had done. *Who am I turning into?* The two reached a lit room, one larger than all the other rooms. Mia's heart rate sped up, even faster than it had been beating before she and Flint had come to an agreement.

"What's this?" she asked, letting her eyes suspiciously wander the area.

"You'll see soon enough. This is where myself and the others were dispatched to help you." He stuck his tongue between his teeth again, grinning broadly, and looked up at the ceiling.

"Hey Tris! Special delivery!"

The light got brighter, and a *bling* like electronic equipment turning on rang through the air. A stairway unfolded from the ceiling, then a trap door appeared out of nowhere. Mia stared as Flint took the first steps up the stairs.

"Um, what?" Mia gaped.

Flint put out his hand, an offer to assist Mia up the steps. "Come and see," he said, urging her to come forward.

Mia took his cool hand, stepping uncertainty onto the staircase. She slowly, very unlike herself, followed Flint up the steps. He opened the trap door and disappeared through it. His hand popped out again a moment later, stretching out for her.

"Let me help you up." Mia looked down. She was by no means afraid of heights, but this high up, her knees did knock together just a little. She looked up again and took Flint's hand.

Flint helped her into a large, rectangular room. The carpet was black, the walls were black, and the ceiling was black. With a *click,* the staircase folded up again, the trap door disappeared, and it was like it had never been there.

"Welcome, Mia! Welcome at last!" Mia's head snapped up so hard she kinked her neck. Rubbing it, her eyes landed on a large desk, in front of which were many, many wall-mounted computers. Most showed smaller screens of different rooms in the maze; some showed other information. And there, in the large office chair, sat Tris, her hair down now, reaching halfway down her back. She was in a long, black dress that had spaghetti straps holding it up. Both eyes were coated in black eyeshadow, though it was smeared over her left eye,like she had accidentally rubbed it, forgetting she had put eyeshadow on. "My darling!" Tris got up, and Mia noticed the woman had on black lace gloves that

158

went all the way to her elbows. She approached Mia in clicking black heels, arms open for an embrace.

Mia, unsure of herself, returned the embrace awkwardly. "You-you..." she stuttered.

"I what, my dear?" Tris asked, giving Mia a winning smile, brushing some hair out of her face as she did so.

"But you're not on my side." Mia backed up until she bumped into Flint. When he put a reassuring hand on her shoulder, she glanced at him gratefully.

"Yes, as a matter of fact, I am," Tris said, twirling with her hands up in the air.

Mia's eyebrow rose, skeptical at this woman's intentions. "Right..." Mia trailed off.

"She's alright, Mia," Flint said.

"Okay, so... How do I get out of here?" she asked.

"Oh, I don't think you need to rush out on us just yet," Tris said, smiling. She turned. "Maria!"

Maria came slowly, Emmitt at her side, out from a dark corner. She was now dressed in a black dress with white dots, her hair up and tied with a black bow. She gave Mia a sheepish smile.

"I knew you were trouble!" Mia bellowed, pointing her finger at the ground in anger as she spoke. Maria's smile disappeared, and she ducked her head.

"Oh, she's no trouble at all," Tris cooed. "We need to learn our manners now, don't we?"

"Our *manners?* What are you talking about?" Mia snarled, beginning to mistrust this woman once again. "We must grant you a gift. You've worked so hard," Maria said, taking a slow step forward. Emmitt stuck to Maria's side. Flint gave Mia's shoulder a gentle squeeze.

"What?" Mia asked, confusion sweeping through her. What was going on here? She was getting mixed signals. There was no way that this woman was… was on her side, right? Right? Maria stepped closer to Mia. "May I take your hand?" Maria asked, looking up at Mia with her big eyes.

Mia shook her head. "No. No, I'd rather you not."

"But how, then, am I to give you the gift?" Maria asked, looking down and scuffing her foot. Her hand slipping into her dress pocket as she did so.

Flint's hand ran down Mia's left arm, catching her hand and cupping it in his. "It's okay, Mia. Trust me." He leaned against her as he guided, with no resistance, her hand towards Maria. Maria gave a little smile, averting her eyes from the two, and withdrew something from her pocket that Mia could not see.

Mia's eyes were drawn to whatever Maria was holding, until something distracted her. She glanced down at Flint's hand. Something about it felt so right where it was. She had never held hands with a man before, but something about Flint was different. Her eyes glanced towards Maria as her hand drew towards Mia's.

Suddenly, something hard and metal clamped on Mia's hand. The gleaming metal claw was digging into her hand.

Mia shrieked, trying to shake it off, and then all at once it was gone. Mia panted, looking at Tris, who had the slightest smirk on her face. The woman quickly swept the smile off her face.

"What was that?" Mia asked, her eyes moving from Tris to Flint, then to Maria. Maria stepped back, sliding both hands into her pockets.

"Oh, just a little present," Tris said coolly.

Mia's eyes flicked to her hand to examine. There were the tiniest of needle marks in each of her fingers. She didn't know what to think. She turned to look at Flint, ready to tell him off for making her trust him so. How dare he trick her?

"Mia, I don't know, honest," Flint said, his eyes wide as he stared at Mia. *Right, right, he 'didn't know.'* Mia shook her head, cradling her hand before realizing how weak that was. She folded her arms, turning back to Tris, anger once more coursing through her.

"How dare you! How dare you do something like that to me! How dare you trap me and my friends! How dare! How… dare…" Mia looked down at her hand, confused. *What am I so angry about, anyways?* She looked back at Flint. *Oh my, he is so handsome.*

Why did she just think that?

She took in his spiky hair, the hair that made Flint, Flint. She smiled broadly at him, taking his hand again before facing Tris.

Tris grinned at her. "Welcome, my dear."

Maria smiled at her. "What a warm greeting indeed," she said.

Mia's uneasiness ebbed away, like she had never felt it. Now she knew who she was. Now she knew why she was here. This was it. The place that she belonged.

Chapter 25

"**Now**, our next step," Tris said, walking daintily towards Mia, "is to get the others to quit fighting. Why would they want to fight after spending their whole lives fighting? Oh! And I've forgotten, I've got a wardrobe change for you!" Seemingly out of nowhere, Tris produced a long black dress, nearly identical to her own but with sleeves, and white trim around the bodice.

Mia's eyes went wide. She had never been a dress person. She had actually never even thought about wearing a dress. Mia couldn't help but reach for it.

But I hate dresses.

Mia ignored herself.

"Oh! My goodness! Thank you!"

"There is a room over there to change," Tris said, nodding towards the left side of the room.

Mia skipped over, finding the door handle and slipping inside with one more glance over to Flint. He was so gorgeous; she couldn't get over it. She shut the door finding herself in a small dressing room, discarding her shirt onto the floor. She slipped off her pants, then pulled the long, silky dress over herself.

Something about the dress built her confidence. She looked in the mirror and grimaced at her mussed up hair. Her hair was never in perfect shape, but it had never been this bad before. She looked around the little room and spotted a hairbrush just sitting there. *Perfect!* She picked it up and began brushing her hair with more care than she normally would. Once her hair shined, she found a hair tie in the dress's pocket. She pulled it out, tugging her hair up into a tight ponytail. She posed quickly in front of the mirror before turning and walking into the bigger room again.

Flint's eyes widened as Mia walked in.

"Why, Mia…" Flint walked over, his hands held out for hers. Mia's face opened into a smile, and she took his hands, gazing into his eyes with a giddy smile creeping onto her face.

"Now, why don't you go help the others?" Tris asked.

"Really?" Mia turned hopefully to Tris. "The others?" *Her friends, right? Obviously, it must be!*

"Yes! Go now, and may your progress exceed expectations!"

The trap door reappeared, and Flint and Mia made their way back down the steep, steep stairs.

Chapter 26

"So, um, how do we know how to get back to—oh!" Mia rapidly blinked her eyes, staring forward as shock rang through her body.

"What's wrong?" Flint grinned at her, as if he knew perfectly well what was *wrong*.

In front of her was a bright green line. It showed her a map of the maze. She could *see the maze!*

"Wow," Mia said, turning to Flint in amazement. "Is this how you knew where to go?"

"Yes, yes it is," Flint said, staring deep into her eyes. He took a step towards Mia, eyes still fixated on her. Mia's breathing became heavier, her heart racing in anticipation of—what? *Something.*

"I…" she breathed. She had never felt anything like this before. Something right near her chest fluttered as a butterfly's wings might.

Flint reached out, tucking a hair behind Mia's ear.

She blinked as Flint took a step closer, his breath warm on her face. She closed her eyes for one heartfelt moment. Then Mia's eyes snapped open and she stepped back, allowing her hair to fall over her face.

"Shall we?" Mia asked, looking where the green arrow pointed.

"Yes," Flint said, nodding in the direction that they were to go.

"Okay then." Mia turned, slipping her hand into Flint's. The two started following the bright green arrow.

Mia's mind whirled, having a green light show the way nearly overwhelming her. She didn't know what to do with her newfound... it didn't feel right to call it a blessing, but it seemed like one at the same time. There was nothing she could think of to call this other than—*what?*

Mia blinked rapidly, experimenting with the neon light disappearing, and reappearing, disappearing, and reappearing, again, and again, and again.

"What is this?" she finally asked Flint.

"What do you mean?" Flint asked.

"What has been implanted in me?"

Flint's eyes scrunched up. "Implanted? What do you mean?"

"I was never able to see where I ought to go before, so what did you do to me in order to get this... this..." Mia's eyebrows furrowed together, her brain telling her that *something* was wrong, though she didn't know what. She couldn't see what was wrong with a green light shooting from her brain and showing her where to go. It was totally normal, and why shouldn't she know? Why should she have no idea how to get where she needed to go? It was completely normal.

"Woah," Mia halted.

She saw a change in her mind, she saw—Eli! Eli and Harper, all scrambling together, circling a figure on the floor and protecting it defensively. No, two figures on the ground. Who? Who were they again?

"I see people," Mia said. "In my eyes."

"Ah," Flint said. "I see we are close to our destination, then." He smiled. "Here's what you'll do."

Mia stumbled back, blinking and shaking her head.

"You okay?" Flint asked, concern flashing across his face as Mia's eyes widened.

"I…" Her chest heaved up and down, up and down. "I know what you want me to do!" She shook her head again. "But you never spoke a word!"

Flint grinned. "Helpful, isn't it?" he asked.

Mia nodded, a grin spreading on her face.

"Yeah. Yeah, I'll do it!"

The plan that had just popped into her head was fully plotted, with bullet points and objectives. Every aspect of the plan was within her mind. Mia walked with purposeful steps into the room her friends were in, a light one.

Eli spotted her first, freezing. Mia's eyes slid to the floor to see who Eli and Harper were protecting.

"Mia?" Eli asked, his voice cautious.

Travis. Travis was on the floor clutching his leg, face twisted in pain. Silvia kneeled at his side, attempting to soothe him.

Harper whirled around, her mouth turning into an O as her eyes met Mia's.

"Mia?" she gasped, similar to Eli's reaction to seeing her.

"Harper." Mia smiled, her eyes dancing with joy. "I found you again!" The cheesy words slipped from her tongue as if she used them all the time.

Harper's eyes narrowed, her posture stiffening.

"Come." Mia held her hand out to her friend.

Harper eyed her. "Mia, what's wrong with you?" she asked.

"What's wrong with me?" Mia gave a tinkling laugh.

Eli stared.

"Nothing is wrong with me, dear," Mia said.

Harper's eyes widened. "What has happened to you?"

"What do you mean?" Mia asked, slipping her hands into her dress pockets and leaning casually against the wall.

"You... What are you wearing, exactly?" Eli butted in, stepping next to Harper defensively.

Mia looked down. "Oh, this old thing? It's nothing! I'm just so glad to have found you!" The words easily slid off her tongue, as if she had spent hours rehearsing them.

"Found us..." Eli trailed off.

"And how *exactly* did you find us?" Harper asked, crossing her arms.

"Does it really matter?" Mia asked, spreading her arms out wide, smiling at her friends. Her *friends!* She had found them at last and could take them into her home, welcoming them with open arms, putting them at ease and showing them just how wonderful this place could be!

"Please! Please, welcome, welcome!" Mia said, striding towards Harper to give her an embrace. Eli stepped in front of Harper, hands on his hips.

"Mia?" Silvia rose, noticing the confrontation. She rose from her protective hovering over Travis's injured body, her eyes lingering on her friends. "What's wrong with you?" Silvia asked.

"Wrong with me?" Mia looked down, then back at her friends, still smiling, still receiving no greeting. How dare they not greet her? "My dears, there is nothing, absolutely *nothing,* wrong with me at all!"

"Mia, stop!" Eli yelled, stepping towards her.

Mia let her feet give herself some personal space. That boy had never had much sense.

"Stop what?" Mia asked, confused on why Eli and Harper were not welcoming her back. She was doing nothing wrong. She needed Flint's help to convince them. *Flint!* she called in her mind. She needed his help to convince them this was the right place. This was obviously the right place. There was no other place to live than right here with Tris. That should be obvious to anyone with a lick of logical sense. "It's just a beautiful place we've got here, don't you think?" she asked, stalling for time. She knew Flint was coming to her rescue, she just knew it.

"Why are you acting like you own the place?" Harper asked, squinting at Mia. "Are you ill or something?"
"Something's up," Eli said. "We have to help her." "How?" Harper asked.

"Mia?" Silvia asked again, stepping forwards so she was in front of Eli.

Mia looked at Silvia. "Silvia!" she said, grinning.

"Mia, you're not right in the head."

That hurt! It was not like Silvia at all to insult her like that. Silvia never told lies or insulted anybody if she could help it!

"No, no. I'm perfectly fine!" Mia insisted. She felt a hand on her back, then Flint was there by her side, his arm slung around her shoulder.

With a clang, Eli drew his sword. "Mia, step away," he warned, his blade pointed threateningly at Flint.

How dare he threaten Flint like that?

"What did Flint ever do to you?" Mia spat, stepping protectively in front of Flint, not unlike how Eli had stepped in front of Harper.

Eli's eyes turned stormy. "Mia. Mia, how could you betray us?" he asked, stepping back, bumping into Harper. "I thought we were starting to get along,"

"Mia, what happened? We are friends. We are friends!" Harper said, a tear sliding down her cheek. *Great!* Mia's mind whined. *She is crying again!*

"Nothing happened to me. I don't know what you all are talking about, and I don't understand why you are all being so mean to me," Mia said, crossing her arms.

Flint's hand on her shoulder softened her tone just the bit. "Cautious with them, my girl. They are little ants in the present of greatness." *What are ants again?* The back of Mia's mind asked at the words Flint had whispered into her ear.

"Mia!" Silvia strode forward and slapped her friend across the face.

Chapter 27

Mia was aghast. In all her life, Silvia had never so much as laid a finger on her—no, that was a lie. Not in all her life. Silvia used to be the enemy after all. But in all the time she had been friends with Mia, slapping someone was the last thing Mia imagined Silvia capable of.

"Don't lay a hand on her." Flint advanced, drawing his weapon, but Eli was there, aggressively stepping in front of Silvia. "Back off, boy," Flint snarled. "Let me at the girl, and you'll have nothing else to fear."

Mia drew her nunchuck from the pocket she kept it in, ready to defend Flint if he needed assistance. *Only* if he needed assistance. This meeting was not going according to plan. Everything was falling apart, and Mia didn't understand why her friends didn't greet her with open arms as they had done when they first found her here.

"Silvia, what's going on?" Travis staggered to his feet, clutching at his leg with his face screwed up in pain. "It's Mia. Look at her, she's not right."

Eli and Flint were still standing off against each other, threatening to go to war. One faked a dart forward, the other raising his weapon to defend himself.

"Mia?" Travis gaped.

Mia wanted to scream. What was with everybody being stunned at her? She was getting really sick of it.

"Mia, get over here and away from that boy."

He dares call Flint a boy! He is a man! A fine man too!

"Travis, how dare you insult Flint?"

"How dare you betray us?" Travis shot back at her.

Mia didn't understand what was going wrong. Her friends never acted like this towards her! There was no reason for them to be angry at her! She was just doing her job.

"Betray you? How could I ever betray you?" Mia gasped, clasping a hand dramatically to her chest.

With a clash of swords, Flint and Eli were on each other, fighting furiously.

"Flint!" Mia cried, going to his aid. She tried to pull him away from Eli.

"Eli!" Harper went to hold Eli back. The two boys shook off their peace makers, fighting to get at each other with vengeful anger.

"Flint, remember our plan," Mia begged. "No one is supposed to be hurt, right?" Just egg them on until they settled with this place as their home, as Mia had come to realize.

Harper and Silvia managed to pull Eli back, his chest heaving. Harper had a firm grip on Eli's sword hand, pulling it down.

"Flint, baby, we must be cautious with this lot," Mia said, crooning to him as she brushed her hand through his hair.

His eyes flashed, but only for a moment. "You're right," he said in a gruff voice.

Mia turned Flint to face her and kissed him, full on the mouth.

There was the clatter of a sword, and all was stunned silence for one, two, three as the new lovers made their thoughts for each other known.

Mia pulled back first, staring deep into Flint's eyes. The realization of what she had been missing her whole life ramming into her like a truck would ram into somebody. She glanced over at Eli, his sword laying at his feet. At Harper, who swayed as if she were about to faint. To Silvia, whose mouth was agape.

Mia's eyes slid back to Flint, and she grinned sheepishly, giving a nervous laugh.

"Wow," Flint said, licking his lips and staring into her soul. "Wow." She could feel his body trembling, her arms still around his neck.

"We must be cautious, baby," she said again, her voice low. "We need to be careful." She ran her thumb down his cheek.

His lips twitched before he pulled away to face Mia's friends.

"You heard her, didn't you?" he asked. "She's doing this for your own good." Flint sheathed his sword.

Harper took a step back, her knees quaking visibly.

Eli's gaze didn't move from the spot where, just moments ago, Mia had been with Flint.

"I've got nothing more to say to you." Silvia turned and buried her face in Travis's neck, her shoulders shaking.

"I…" Eli's voice failed him. He didn't seem like his brain could work anymore, the way he stood there. His eyes were still fixated on the spot.

"Come with us," Mia urged, ignoring the stunned silence of her friends. "I'll show you a better life."

"Mia," Harper whispered. "Mia, this isn't you." Harper obviously wanted to change Mia's mind, when it was Harper who needed her mind fixed.

"Yes, this is me," Mia said, straightening her shoulders and clasping Flint's hand again. "I don't know why you are all so shocked."

"No. Mia, come back to us." Harper stepped toward her. "Come back to you?" Mia gasped. "You are the ones who walked away from me," she insisted, giving Harper a cold look. "You abandoned me!"

"Mia, you've got it all wrong." Harper grabbed Mia's free hand, tugging it.

"No, Harper," Eli said, his eyes ablaze. He grabbed Harper's free hand, pulling her back.

"No! Eli, we can't give up on her!" Tears streamed down Harper's face.

Mia tightened her grip on Flint's hand, determined not to let her friends pull her into the other side, the side against Flint. *How could anybody be against Flint?*

"Harper, she's done for." Eli's eyes had slid to Mia's hand clamped tightly in Flint's. A choked sob ripped from him, one Mia had never heard from his mouth before.

"No, no she's not!" Harper sobbed. "We can't give up on her, Eli! I know she's still in there!" Harper let go of Mia, spinning to face him.

"You can't let her go!"

In a flash, Mia was on top of Harper, wrapping her hands around her neck and squeezing. Harper's mouth opened wide like a fish's, her hair brushing against Mia's cheek. Mia pulled her back, dragging Harper's feet along the ground.

"Mia!" Eli bellowed, launching forward in attack mode.

But Mia was too fast. She whirled about, thrusting Harper into Flint's arms, who put a sword up against her throat as she spluttered and gasped for air.

"That," Mia gasped, panting from the excitement and thrill the action had given her, "is what happens to people who cross us!"

Mia's eyes blazed at Eli, Travis, and Silvia, daring them to contradict her. She pointed to Harper. "Any sudden movement and she dies! You hear me? She dies!"

Chapter 28

Nobody moved. Eli's gaze was fixed on Harper's gasping face. Silvia leaned against Travis, as if she didn't know how to express her shock of having Mia threaten the life of a lifelong friend. Mia knew this was a normal thing to do. If someone didn't behave, someone else paid. It was the way of life, and there was no reason whatsoever for her friends to be shocked.

Mia grinned. "There, now we get it, don't we?" Mia said cooly, letting her satisfied gaze linger on Eli's stunned expression.

"We get what, exactly? What is it we are supposed to understand?" Eli asked.

Oh! This boy!

Mia tensed. "You—"

Flint came to Mia's rescue. "Understand that we are safe here. This is where we ought to be. Now relax, why don't ya?" He jiggled the sword pressed against Harper's throat playfully.

"How is this place in any way a home?" Silvia stepped forward, her tear-stained face a mask of hopelessness. "Mia, we came to save you! To *save* you!"

"No, we came to save ourselves," Mia contradicted. "That's why we brought you all here! To protect you from the outside world!"

"No, Mia. You're not making sense. You're not talking sense!"

"It's okay that you don't understand yet," Mia said soothingly.

"Harper will understand, as I do, soon enough."

"You will do nothing to her!" Eli snapped, stepping towards Mia. "Take me instead."

"Oh!" Mia laughed. "How noble of you to assume we would do a trade! But Harper here, this dear is just too precious to let go. I don't see why we would ever let her go." Mia stepped over to her friend and placed a hand on her head, affection for her good friend Harper filling her close to bursting.

"Get off me!" Harper said so fiercely a ragged cough erupted from her.

Mia looked at her, slightly amused. "Why Harper, don't you see? You are finally safe with Flint and me," she said, bending down to look Harper in the eyes as she might a little kid.

Harper snapped at her. Mia jumped back, disgusted. What was going through her mind to cause her to do such a silly little thing?

"Now now, dear," Mia said. "We don't bite Ms. Mia, do we? We get dangerous consequences for disobeying the rules."

"What rules?"

Mia spun around, finding herself face to face with Eli.

"The rules," Mia said, having no idea what the rules were—she came up with them as they went along, for there were definitely rules around here.

"You're making them so clear to us. Let Harper go! It's three against two," he reminded Mia.

"Oh, well, thank you for the reminder," Mia said. *Hey Flint, we ought to call for backup.*

As you wish, my darling.

"The reminder? You are out of your mind! We are—hang on, let me rephrase that—we were your friends!" Eli said, his face contorting with pain. "Mia! Snap out of it, now!"

"I think not."

They are a little busy right now, babes, but Blade will join us if he can slip away.

Gotcha!

"Come on," Mia purred. "You don't really think I've changed that much, do you?"

Eli opened his mouth, appearing to be speechless, but then managed, "You think you haven't changed?"

Mia's eyes scrunched up. "You're not making sense. Flint, let's go."

"Give Harper back first!" Eli insisted. "Mia, please."

"No, why should I?" Mia asked, her hands clenching into fists in exasperation. He was being insufferable!

"Because… because you've got to! Because we must escape!" Eli spluttered.

"Mia, listen to us, please," Travis said.

"Shut up," Mia snapped. "Shut up, or it'll be worse for you!" She raised her voice.

Eli opened his mouth again, as if threatening to say something, but then stopped. He shook his head. Mia noticed a tear glinting in his eyes. She scrunched up her nose, turning her back on him. She waved to Flint, who dragged a struggling Harper out of the lit room and into blackness.

Chapter 29

The blackness did not bother Mia anymore. She could see perfectly well in the dark with her upgrade. She couldn't imagine not having it.

"What's up guys?" Blade stood in front of them, eyes dancing in mischief.

"We can't let them hear us." Mia jutted her head to the doorway they'd just come through, Harper struggling along the way. Flint clapped a hand over Harper's mouth, and she went limp, side-eyeing Mia more than ever before.

An enraged scream reached Mia's ears as they walked into another room. "Mia! Mia, how dare you!" It was Eli's voice, full of grief.

"I never could have imagined!" Silvia's raised voice was petrified with something Mia couldn't figure out. Then they had moved out of earshot, still dragging a resigned Harper along with them.

"Where to?" Mia asked. "We can't report back to Tris without good news."

"We have good news, though," Flint said, jerking Harper up and wrapping an arm around her neck.

"Let me take her," Blade pleaded. "I want to give her a try." He smiled.

Flint shoved Harper so that she fell into Blade's arms. She looked up at Mia as Blade grabbed her shirt, a smile spreading across his face.

"Well, well, a feisty one, aren't we?" he asked, admiring Harper's shiny black hair.

"Mia." Harper's voice was pleading, babyish.

"What, my friend?" Mia asked, not understanding why Harper appeared so frightened.

"What are you doing?"

Mia was stunned. Harper had clearly lost her mind, and there was no way Mia could get through to her. She would have to use blunt force.

"There is no explaining logic to you, now, is there?" Mia asked, staring deeply at her.

"Logic? *Logic?* You call kidnapping your own friends, the friends who tried to save you, logic?" Tears began streaming down Harper's face again. *My gosh, what a baby!*

"There's no use. I'll have to take you to the boss!" Mia sang, turning away and looking at her pals.

"Ready, Flint?"

"Ready," Flint said, his face bright with anticipation.

"Let's take her then." Mia marched along the path, the way of the green line.

Chapter 30

The way was quick, the fight from Harper nonexistent. It was as if Harper had lost all hope of returning to the enemy's side. She seemed to have finally decided to stick with Mia and her new friends. Her feet resignedly carried her along, Blade's fist still clenching a handful of her shirt.

"Now the way is so clear, don't you see, Harper?" Mia asked. "All you must do is comply with our will and we will treat you well."

"Your will? *Your* will? I thought your will was to escape this monstrous hole in this random place! What's gotten int—"

Mia interrupted Harper, refusing Harper's foolish thoughts to play with her sanity.

"Something has gotten into you, my dear. There is much wrong with you that we must fix."

"Stop calling me dear," Harper snapped. *That sounds familiar...* But Mia couldn't place it. All she knew was she *must,* absolutely *must,* get Harper on her side! Without Harper, one of the best fighters she knew, she didn't know what she'd do. Without her best friend... But she did have Flint now. Flint would stick next to her even if Harper had the audacity to abandon her. "Well, you are following step one quite nicely," Mia commented to avoid Harper's anger.

"Step one?"

"Yes. Come with us willingly."

"When is being held captive by your friend, or enemy, called willingly! Where has your logical mind gone?" "Logic is always with me, sweetie." Harper clamped her lips shut.

The way back to Tris's entrance felt long, especially now that Harper was refusing to talk to her. Friends were supposed to talk to each other, talk and have a good time. Obviously. So now that Harper was being so stubborn, Mia was frustrated. Why was Harper angry with her, anyway? She had no right to be so angry! Mia was about to change Harper's life for the better! Harper was much safer in here, after all, than she was out there in the blazing sun, with those cars buzzing by at mind speed and the people who always stared at those useless flat things! There were years of freedom for all of them within these walls. No one could convince her otherwise. They were safe here! *Safe, safe, safe!*

The next thing Mia knew, the stairway was lowering, and Blade and Flint were forcing Harper up the stairs. Mia followed them, triumphant in her first capture of an enemy—her friend who had no sense whatsoever and didn't know a comfortable home when she saw one.

Chapter 31

"**Welcome!**" Tris's friendly voice chirped as Mia's head appeared into the dark office again, computer screens blinking this way and that. "Welcome back, my dear!" Tris walked forward and embraced Mia. Mia hugged her back so exuberantly she appeared to take even Tris by surprise. "Why, I see it's set in brilliantly!" She looked to Flint. "No trouble then, I take it?"

Flint shook his head. "None at all."

Blade shoved Harper forwards as the staircase returned to its resting spot. Harper stared coldly at Tris, not her usual expression at all. She was usually timid, meek, but now her rare, ferocious side seemed to be seeping out at the seams.

"Good evening dear," Tris said to Harper, her eyes appraising her appearance. "You need a wardrobe change as well."

"What do you mean?" Harper said, her grammar slipping up in all the confusion. Mia pitied her. She understood what it was like to be scared, to be taken, but Harper ought to know she was in good hands here. Harper was with people who cared for her.

"What I mean, my dear…" Tris gave a tinkling laugh. A red flashing light caught Mia's attention from one of the computers, and her eyes scanned the screens, her eyes narrowing. "I mean that you need help."

"Obviously!" Harper said, rolling her eyes.

"You need help finding the way. Maria!"

Harper's eyes widened. "What do you—" Harper stopped herself and gaped as Maria entered the room from… somewhere, some entrance that Mia wasn't able to see. Emmitt was at her side, his ears forward, head held high.

"Harper!" Maria said, smiling broadly.

Mia's eyes flickered back to the screens, searching frantically. They showed live footage from each room in the maze, light and dark alike, the technology being advanced enough to show what was happening in the darkest of rooms. There were Brynlee and Joseph, both fighting Gale—it took two to fight her; she was a strong woman—then more rooms as a group on Mia's side ran through the maze, running to or from something Mia couldn't tell. Then, her eyes found—

"Let me go, you crook!" Harper flung herself at Tris, but both Flint and Blade stepped forwards in one movement, grabbing each of Harper's shoulders and pulling the struggling girl back. Mia noticed Blade surreptitiously slipping the bag of daggers off of Harper. She appeared not to notice as she glowered at Tris.

"You'll pay for this, mark my words! Why do you want us, anyway? Can't you just leave us alone?"

"No, we can't leave you alone, my dear. You see, you are too precious for us."

That got Mia's attention. Tris hadn't told *her* she was precious. She had told *her* it was safe here. A sprout of jealousy began blistering within Mia. Her eyes flitted back to the screen with the flashing red light.

"Hold on a moment." Tris made her way to the computers, tapping on the screen so the room Eli, Silvia, and Travis were in was full screen. She saw Eli staring directly into the camera. He had somehow figured out how to find the camera lens.

"Oh, deary." Tris sighed, pressing a button. A steaming cup of coffee popped out of the wall. Fatigue suddenly gripped Mia, but she couldn't let it show. She couldn't let anyone see how tired and hungry she was. Tris took a sip as she clicked another button, and the security footage showed the TV screen pulled down again, revealing Tris's face to her friends. Her friends down there stared at the TV. "Well, well, if it isn't my favorite trio!"

"What have you done with Harper?" Eli snarled, stepping towards the TV.

"I'll show you how safe she is." Tris turned, lowering her voice. "Blade, bring her forward, but don't let the camera pick you up."

Blade shoved Harper forwards.

"Harper!" Silvia yelled. "Please tell me they've done nothing to you!"

"Oh, not yet, my dear," Tris said.

Harper attempted to run at the camera, but Blade held her back.

"Silvia, help! Mia's mind's not right! Something's different. Wrong. I—"

Blade jerked her back, slapping his hand over her mouth and letting his fingernails dig into her soft flesh. Harper struggled against Blade's grip, but his strong frame overpowered her with ease.

"Let her go!" Eli shouted, raising his fist at the screen.

Tris chuckled. "You silly little things, when will you learn?" she asked, raising an eyebrow.

"Where is Mia?" Eli snarled. Eli was not one to snarl. Mia had to know why he did it. She shoved her way into the screen, looking down on Eli with contempt.

"Mia! We will escape, but I don't know if you'll come with us."

Well, that was just fine with Mia. Mia didn't want to go with them. The traitors.

"You will never escape!" Mia yelled. Tris stepped back, letting Mia have her moment of rage. It was fierce, and it boiled up inside her so she could not contain it any longer. Her friends were not being fair! Her friends were the traitors, not her.

"You will live here in safety! We can't have people like you running wild on the streets!" Mia yelled.

"Like 'you'?" Eli repeated, appalled.

"Eli, chill," Travis said, limping forwards painfully.

"Yes, like you!" Mia said. "And now, if you don't mind, I have more important things to do than argue with you." Mia moved so her whole face blocked the screen, letting her eyes dig into Eli's with hatred as never before. "I'm out!" Mia punched the screen, and it flickered black.

Mia turned to Tris, rage coursing through her veins so much she trembled.

"Mia?" Harper's soft voice reached her ringing ears.

"What?" Mia snapped at her.

"Mia, please."

"No, no, I don't think so." Mia turned to Tris. "What's next?"

Tris smiled. "I thought you'd never ask."

Mia smiled, pulling her ponytail out and running her hand through her hair. She glanced at the screen, where she could see the others staring at the blank space where the projection had just been. She was pleased with her performance and how things had gone. She was ready for the next level, the next challenges. She was ready to tackle them with Flint.

She had never imagined she would be in love with a man, or anyone for that matter, but Flint had her head over heels. She leaned over and kissed him, their lips moving in unison for one, two, three blissful moments before she pulled away, gazing into his green eyes.

"So, my lady," Flint said, sticking his tongue through the gap in his teeth and looking over at Tris. "What's next, as Mia asked?"

Tris smiled, a bit of black lipstick marring her white teeth. "We have some psychology games to play, and I think it'll be a fun way to, well, to welcome our new friends home. A good way to keep things moving in section C."

"What's section C?" Mia asked, her eyes flitting from Flint's wonderfully gorgeous eyes to Tris's.

"When you're ready, you'll learn about section C. It's classified for now. You'll learn eventually, once you prove you're worth it."

Something swelled up inside Mia. If she had to prove her worth, she would. She was worth more than Maria, Emmitt, and all her old friends combined! She didn't need anyone other than Flint, who could protect her better than anyone she knew. He was stronger than she was, something she had never imagine admitting to herself. It was a start.

This was the start of something new. She needed to find out what section C was. She would prove herself worthy. And she would do it with Flint by her side.

The End

www.ingramcontent.com/pod-product-compliance
Lightning Source LLC
Chambersburg PA
CBHW051956220626
47052CB00004B/968